MW00949246

"Hernon's plot is filled with constant twists and turns and un-clichéd scenes. And, while there is no doubt that locals, as well as horror and phantasmal aficionados, will love this new addition to Manhattan ghost stories, *In the Shadow of St. Anthony* is one of those stories that would be great on the silver screen."

-San Francisco Book Review

"A more literary and well-rounded entry into the horror genre."

-Self-Publishing Review

"In the Shadow of St. Anthony is a wonderful novel. It will be interesting to see what Andrew Hernon gives us in the future."

-Portland Book Review

"The author, Andrew Hernon, truly brings the feelings, sights, and smells of this neighborhood alive, from the heat radiating off of the cement to the smell of Tommy's signature sauce. *In the Shadow of St. Anthony* is at once a horror novel, but also the portrait of a community, insulated by its history and geography, people just struggling to get by and find their places in a scary, unknown world."

-Manhattan Book Review

IN THE SHADOW OF ST. ANTHONY

Being a somewhat detailed account of
the coming of age of Tommy Santalesa,
the neighborhood wiseass.

ANDREW HERNON

Copyright © 2015 Andrew Hernon
All rights reserved.

ISBN: 1508651892
ISBN 13: 9781508651895
Library of Congress Control Number: 2015903301
CreateSpace Independent Publishing Platform
North Charleston, South Carolina

ACKNOWLEDGMENTS

I'd like to thank the following wonderful people for their help with this book. My wife, Nancy who had to deal with all my indecision, hand wringing, and worry. In short, without her this never would have gotten finished.

Elizabeth Leonard, for her insights, priceless encouragement and friendship.

Deborah Emin, for the instruction and guidance in the early days.

Phoebe M. West and Rachel Kempf for awesome copy editing, and excellent proof reading in addition to being two pairs of much needed objective eyes

Eric Sherman for helping me wake up.

For Ellen, my mother.
We had a great thirty-five years together.

"Well now everything dies baby, that's a fact
But maybe everything that dies someday comes back."
- Bruce Springsteen, "Atlantic City"

PROLOGUE

Around here the old Italians used to tell you not to go west of Sixth Avenue after the sun went down. The printing district, wedged between Varick Street and the West Side Highway, from Houston to Canal, was a no man's land at the end of the workday. After five p.m. the place would clear out faster than roaches running for cover in a basement at the flip of a light switch. It was just one block west of Sixth Avenue.

One night in the summer of 1982, two vagrants, Jenny the Lush and Greasy Fred, sat on the courtyard loading dock in the rear of 50 Van Dam Street taking swigs from a bottle of cheap liquor. Police sirens rose and fell like crashing waves in the background. Their legs dangled over the side as their feet swayed a little more than a foot and a half above the asphalt. Steam practically rose off the cement and the air was so thick and muggy it was like wearing wool. Still, it was never busy in *that* part of the city at night. No residents and, more importantly, no cops to hassle them.

Greasy Fred wriggled and then slid off his seat on the loading dock.

"Where are *you* going?" Jenny asked with slurred words and a jerky pointing gesture. It came off as an accusation.

"To take a piss," he said with a scowl as he wandered away in a sloppy swagger into a darker spot of the courtyard. He reached a patch of dead grass by a warped and weathered chain-link fence on the other side and unzipped his pants.

The area was a haven for people like them in the summer, but that night it seemed particularly dead. Jenny wondered if the regular gang had acted on her idea of spending a few hours out of the heat in an air-conditioned movie theater. The Ziegfeld up on 54th Street was playing a revival of *The Muppet Movie,* and she always got a kick out of hearing the goofs in the back row of the balcony shout, "Bring out the bear, bring out the bear!"

In the distance, car horns blared and brakes screeched while bloated gray clouds covered the island of Manhattan like a down comforter.

A darkened blotch, camouflaged by the night, glided over the blacktop. If any person had seen it, they would have watched it slide along the ground, temporarily paint itself on the curb made of cobblestone, and then become a moving blemish on the face of the asphalt.

A fat cockroach, the size of a mouse, sensed the approaching shadow and scampered nervously away where it slipped between the bars of a metal sewer grate. A cluster of rats nearby were even poised to dart in the opposite direction as it moved past them. It reached the path's edge and, like water, assumed the shape of the curb then disappeared again into the blacktop.

She caught a vague reflection of her face in a small puddle by her side. Vague as her reflection was, it told the truth. She looked at least seven years older than her real age of twenty-nine. If the same rule applied to Greasy Fred, then the mileage on his face said he was over fifty.

Jenny needed a distraction, so she looked over her shoulder at the building, an abandoned redbrick structure, and fixed her eyes on its rear door. It was an old, heavy, and brooding rectangular slab of metal that had an air of being definite and final. She adjusted her position and rose to her feet. She flicked her cigarette off into the darkness and raised the bottle to her lips. She stood directly in front of the door and wondered then, as she often had, what was behind it.

The 1 train rumbled beneath Varick Street as it headed south to Canal Street.

She looked back again but couldn't see Greasy Fred in the dark patch he had stepped into and it made her nervous. Despite the numbing effects of the alcohol, she wasn't comfortable there by herself.

She knew the rumors about the area and what the old Italians on the other side of Sixth Avenue said about *this* side of the neighborhood after dark.

But those were just rumors.

Jenny was relieved as Greasy Fred stepped out of the dark and into a small pool of weak light from a street lamp outside the courtyard. As he walked he zipped his pants. Then he stopped, fumbled to strike a match to light the cigarette between his lips.

Something moved very quickly and caught her eye.

In an instant Greasy Fred was gone. He disappeared with only a weak and muffled yelp.

Did he fall? Was it a trick of the light, or did she actually see a wad of black, like an oily blanket, rise behind Greasy Fred and pounce on him? She called out to him. Her voice cracked and went momentarily silent. Her eyes darted as she got the courage to call out again. This time she yelled, almost screamed his name.

Nothing.

Now she was sure she saw something like a puddle, jiggling with ripples, move from the spot where Greasy Fred had just stood. She watched it slide down the side of the cobblestone curb where it was lost in the blacktop.

From her position on the loading dock, her eyes strained to follow it, but she spotted the black splotch as it glided on the asphalt across the courtyard in her direction. Like a woman in a boat watching a shark's approaching fin, she stepped back from the loading dock's ledge in shock.

When her eyes lost it again, she stepped forward and looked down from the ledge but saw nothing below but the blacktop.

Something innate told Jenny to step back. Then, from its camouflaged state on the ground, it sprang up at her. She jumped back and stumbled, but never took her eyes off the shadowy mass as it spread out before her toes on the concrete loading dock.

The bottle fell from her hand and shattered on the ground. Jenny turned to run and lost her footing. She jumped in fear and shock as she felt an intensely painful grip in her underarms. Suddenly, she was violently pulled backward.

Her head snapped back, and then she was yanked to the ground on her back. She sputtered and kicked like a struggling fly caught in a spider's web. Every muscle in her body became tense from fear. Like a deliberate and slow-moving wave, the shadow overtook her. Some voice in the back of her mind whispered that her attempt to escape was futile, and was vindicated as the grip on her tightened. She felt a pierce in her neck, and then calmness came over her. It was a feeling of euphoria as her fear and tension were drained. She wondered, as her mind faded, if she was in water. She remembered once hearing that people drowning feel almost high as they check out. Her hands and feet grew cold. Something dug into her chest and she gave out an amused chuckle as if it wasn't really happening.

Her vision faded and the last thing she saw was a gaping hole in her chest as the shadow moved away and slid beneath the heavy steel door of the redbrick structure.

PART ONE
BIGGER THAN ZEPPELIN

CHAPTER 1

Tommy Santalesa's size-fourteen, beat-up, and dingy off-white Pro-Keds pounded out a heavy beat as they slapped the sidewalk. He bounced a blue rubber handball in time with the beat. In his other hand, he clutched an enormous sandwich made of scrambled eggs, cheese, and potatoes stuffed into a Portuguese roll. There were gaps in the beat between the strides of his long legs. About a year earlier, when he was eighteen, he peaked at just an inch over six feet in height. His brown hair was grown out in a shoulder-length bush. Shirtless and in a pair of faded blue Levi's that hung on to his hips, Tommy lunge-walked across West Broadway along Spring Street with his Van Halen 1981 North American Tour T-shirt flipped over his right shoulder. His eyes, not yet but soon to be blood-shot, were shrouded behind a cheap pair of Aviator sunglasses that he bought from a street vendor over on St. Mark's Place a few weeks before.

He resembled a younger and living, but olive-skinned Jim Morrison.

It was only eleven a.m. and already eighty-nine degrees. The forecast said it would reach ninety-eight later in the day.

With the exception of the weather, which Tommy said ruined his tan, and a new Van Halen album that he wasn't too impressed with, the only other thing that didn't sit right with him was the new singer in Iron Maiden. The lyrics were good and the music was awesome, but Tommy told Moe Martinez, his partner in crime, "This new guy sounds like Ethel Merman, Moe."

Moe thought Tommy was nuts and said that the new singer was going to take Iron Maiden to the next level. Tommy didn't see it and he couldn't wrap his brain around how that band decided to get rid of the original singer in the first place.

Be that as it may, the summer of 1982 had been pretty good to him. His parents were still off on vacation in the old country, so he and his older sister Lisa had the place all to themselves. His parents wouldn't be back for another week, which meant he didn't have to sweat that talk with his father about his standing academic probation or his future.

A week may as well as be a year for all he cared because he had other pressing matters to attend to. Besides, he was going to be a rock star in a few weeks anyway. He, Moe, and Frank were all headed for greatness. Stuffed in the front pocket of his jeans was a dime bag of the finest homegrown from the private stash of Willy Wang, Tommy's hookup over on Bayard Street in Chinatown. Sure, it was a long way there and back from the pizzeria on Bleecker Street, but it was worth it.

He spotted Moe Martinez seated and waiting on a wooden and green-painted bench outside of Thompson Street Park. To Moe's left, on the bench, was a plastic cooler filled with a bag of ice, some plastic cups, a half gallon of orange juice, and an unopened bottle of vodka. To his right was an enormous cassette-deck radio. He wore cutoff shorts, a white tank top, had a red bandanna wrapped around the top of his head, and wore the same cheap sunglasses as Tommy. His shoulder-length black hair was pulled into a ponytail. He held onto a newspaper clipping.

Seeing Tommy at the corner, he folded the newspaper and stuffed it into his back pocket. Then he stood up and tapped his wrist. "Baby, you're late." Moe looked him over. "What were you thinking wearing jeans on a day like this?"

"Cut me some slack, bro," Tommy said. "I had to be in the pizzeria at four thirty this morning to spin out twenty extra pies for Vinny Sr. Oh and I bumped into Aunt Jemima on the way over here. She said to tell you she wants her hat back."

Moe laughed at the jab and didn't miss a beat. "Did they give you a free bowl of soup at the homeless shelter where you got those sneakers from?"

4

They smacked hands as they met. Moe was a good seven inches shorter than Tommy.

After they crossed Sixth Avenue and nearly ten minutes later, they were in their makeshift handball court, an empty lot behind a townhouse that had been converted into a veterinarian's office years before. In addition to there being a smooth and even concrete floor, the lot came with a high, flat, and even cement wall. Best of all, it was on the other side of Sixth Avenue and away from all the neighborhood eyes. Outside of their circle of friends, the only other person that knew about the place was Doc Myers, the veterinarian, and he didn't seem to mind.

"What a morning I've had," Tommy said as a cigarette dangled from his lips. "I had to run out at a quarter to ten, lock the place up, and run all the way down to Bayard Street to meet Willy Wang. I barely made it on time, and you know what a dick he can be if you're late."

"He's just paranoid," Moe said, standing over the open cooler.

"It was worth it though." Tommy pulled a clear plastic sandwich bag from his pocket. He tossed it to Moe. "It's from his private stash."

Moe was in awe, as if he held the Holy Grail. "No shit?"

"Swear to God."

"How did this happen?"

"Don't get me wrong. It came with a price like everything else with him. On top of his normal rate, I had to give him a jar of my sauce and agree to take out his goofy sister."

Moe pictured Vicki Wang's teeth and had to laugh. "Wow! You really took one for the team. You're a better man than me." He went back to the cooler, filled two cups with ice, poured in some orange juice, and then spun the cap off the vodka bottle.

Pouring the vodka into the cups, Moe watched Tommy, who was sitting on his heels as he rolled a joint. Watching Tommy roll was like seeing a master craftsman at work, Moe believed. Tommy was real artist at it because he had an awesome way of tightly rolling a bone. The joints were always skinny, but because of Tommy's intense rolling technique, the intake on a hit was maximized.

"You know what that is?" Tommy asked as held the held the joint up for display between his thumb and middle finger.

"That's precision," Moe said, handing a cup to Tommy. "It's just too bad Frank's not here."

"Why?" Tommy looked at him like he was crazy. "It's just wasted on him, and anyway, he's still moaning over that girl. I haven't seen him for like three days; not since the show. I haven't talked to him since…I don't even know. You?"

"I haven't talked to him since the band meeting the other day. You weren't there."

The other trick Tommy had was to crack the joint in two halves. He'd light the rolled end and pull from the open end. It really made for the most of a hit!

"I had to work, Moe." Tommy said it like Moe didn't know what it meant to work. "I don't get him anyway. I knocked on his window the other day and got no answer. When he gets depressed he vanishes like Houdini." Tommy handed Moe his half of the joint.

You hooked him up with that girl in the first place, Moe thought as he lit the end and took a hit. Rolling a joint was only one of Tommy's gifts. In addition, Tommy had the looks and a good line of bullshit so that he didn't even really have to try too hard with girls. In a band or not, most of the time they just fell over themselves for him. However, Tommy's most notable skill was in the kitchen. Many would swear that Tommy could make cardboard taste incredible and his homemade sauce was nothing short of divine. What troubled Moe was, how could a guy cook so good, roll so good, be that good with his hands, and yet suck so bad at playing the bass?

Moe held his breath and, despite being troubled, thought it was going to be a beautiful day. First, he was getting a taste of Willy Wang's fabled private stash, second, the girls were coming, and third, that beautiful write-up their band got from the *Daily News* was in his back pocket. The sky above was gloomy and overcast, but to Moe the future was looking very bright. He pulled out the latest newspaper clipping from his back pocket. He'd read it so many times he had it memorized, but he still liked reading it.

"We're going to be bigger than Zeppelin, Tommy," Moe said. "It says so here and I quote, 'Catch them at the French Donut before they crack the big time because they are going to be bigger than Led Zeppelin!'"

"That's pretty big," Tommy said flatly.

"You don't seem too impressed with the write-up we got."

Tommy threw the rubber handball off the wall softly. As it returned, he whacked it back to the wall with his palm. "You want the truth?"

"No, I want you to lie." Moe stepped forward and caught the ball midair.

Holding his breath, Tommy said, "It's not my best picture…"

"It's a picture…of us…of our band…in a newspaper. A real newspaper, Tommy. Oh, I get it now. You're just pissed because Frank looks better than you in the picture."

"…and that guy who wrote it…the way he talks about Frank…like, I'm not even mentioned anywhere in it except for where he got my name wrong and calls me Tony Santalesa. Tony? Forget the fact that you guys changed the name of the band to Fly-Trap without even letting me know. Fly-Trap? What does that even mean? It makes me think of that weird plant they sell on channel nine at three in the morning." He finally exhaled and made a bitter face. "I heard the demo, Moe. Vines played it for me. I know you think I'm tone deaf, but I do know that I didn't play any of those bass lines."

"That's because you never bothered to learn them." Moe dug into his other back pocket and handed Tommy a piece of folded white paper.

Tommy glanced at it, rolled his eyes, and handed it back. "You know I can't read this. I barely read tablature."

"How can you call yourself a musician and not be able to read music?" Why anyone wouldn't want to know how to read music was a mystery to Moe.

"That's just it, retard." He snatched the ball from Moe's hand. "I never said I was musician; you and Frank did. I can't…I don't even know what kind of music we play anymore. Whatever happened to playing some old Stones and Black Sabbath stuff?"

Um, we evolved, Moe thought. From the corner of his eye, he saw four girls entering their handball court. His eyes locked onto Donna, a tall, fair-skinned, fair-haired girl with blue eyes. He turned to Tommy and said through gritted teeth, "Don't queer my pitch."

"She's into you, bro. Besides, she's not my type," Tommy said loud enough so that only Moe could hear him.

Everybody else's woman is your type, Tommy, Moe thought as he pulled deeply on his joint. He turned and smiled at the four girls. "Ladies, so nice to see you."

Three of the girls giggled, but not Donna. She stepped to Moe, leaned down as she towered over him, and pressed her lips to his. He blew the smoke into her mouth and gave her the remains of the joint. Then he gestured to the open cooler.

Tommy was done with his joint and handed it off to one of the girls without even looking at her. He slammed the blue ball off the wall. Moe fell in line. The ball took turns being whacked by their palms between hitting the wall.

Then Moe volleyed, and Tommy swung and missed. It was Moe's point.

As the ball rolled away and Tommy went after it, Moe pressed play on the tape deck. For a few moments there was the sound of tape hiss before something loud and heavy exploded through the speakers. Guitars grinded and drums pounded furiously with a bass line that shook the ground. It was one of Moe's mixed tapes, a random collection of hard rock, heavy metal, and punk.

Tommy picked up the handball, faced the wall, and looked up at the gray, bloated clouds. "This weather's screwing up my tan."

Chapter 2

"All aboard! Ha, ha, ha, ha, ha…"

Ozzy Osbourne's wailing voice tore into the office and drilled itself right into Doc Myers's ears with such intensity that his eyelids flew open. His head hurt already, but now it was splitting, too. He wanted to close the window, but was too hung-over to get up and close it.

Myers heard it that morning just like he heard it most mornings that summer. It was the official announcement that those neighborhood kids—the ones that hung out in the back lot to smoke weed and play handball—had arrived.

The filtered sunlight came through the window in a blinding assault that annoyed him. Annoyed him like everything else that morning. A half-full bottle of whiskey was on the desk across from him. It mocked him in the manner that only the insane can understand. He rolled over on his back, shut his eyes, and pinched the bridge of his nose with his thumb and index finger. He heard somewhere doing this helped relieve the pressure. It didn't. His knees ached as they always did when he didn't get enough sleep and his stomach was in knots. To make things worse, he suffered the effects of some migraine-and-sinus-hybrid headache.

He rolled over, planted his feet on the floor, put on his glasses, and took his time standing up. Last thing he needed was to risk a head rush and then fall over. He walked very slowly to the window. He could see them about fifteen feet below him. As usual they brought a cluster of girls with them, and the girls, it seemed, never played handball. They sat on the ground in a row with their backs to an adjacent wall smoking cigarettes, laughing, and smiling. Just the boys played the game, but there were only two of them today, the tall one and the short one. Just then Myers realized he hadn't seen the midsized one for a while.

None of them, the boys or girls, could be older than nineteen, he assumed. They seemed so young to him and so happy. Despite the fact that they were loud, cursed a lot, and loved to blare that radio, Myers found them endearing and envied their youth. He remembered being young and laughing in the summer and not having a care in the world. Then in an instant, he remembered, himself in the jungle, holding an M16.

He eyed the girls left to right and took in their long feathered and layered hair, their long red fingernails, and the tube tops all the girls in the city wore that summer. Each one was prettier than the last. Despite the heat wave and the thick humidity, those girls never seemed to sweat. Most of the time they wore designer jeans with brand names like Sergio Valente, Jordache, or Sasson that fit around their legs and hips snugly to create the perfect picture.

The pounding of high heels on the hardwood floor outside in the hallway snapped him out of his daydream. Each step she took rang out in his head like a church bell.

Of the all the days for her to show up on time!

Myers rounded his desk, placed the bottle of whiskey in the trash can, and took a seat. He leaned back, rested his head against the wall, and shut his eyes.

The office door creaked. He cracked open one eye and caught a glimpse of her carrying something with both hands. He shut his eye and hoped that she might actually believe he was just suffering from a headache.

But he knew better. Cynthia Batista was no fool.

Even with his eyes closed he could see the image of her defined hips as they swayed left to right as she approached the desk. What she lacked in personality most days, she made up for in curves. It was not to say she didn't have a personality, but that she chose to use it depending on whatever mood she was in.

She carried an open cardboard box in front of her. On the top of the box's contents were two manila folders. She plopped the cardboard box down on the desk with a thud. She lifted the two folders and tucked them beneath her arm. "A bowl of cavatelli from Mrs. Lantieri, sauce on the side," she said as she removed it from the box. "Fried zucchini and a bowl of pasta fagioli from Mrs. Cannazarro. Finally, a plate of ziti with a side of tomato and mozzarella from Nona DeNapolitano."

She smelled the booze and knew Al Lucchese had been over the night before. There was a bitter taste in her mouth. Cynthia didn't like Lucchese and she hated the friendship that had grown between him and Myers in the past few months. "Up front is a stack of boxes from Paladino's food market. The deliveryman says it's a gift from Nona Paladino for taking such good care of her granddaughter's cat. I guess you finally have a use for that big freezer you never use." She dropped the folders on the desk. "And the two files you asked for."

Myers's eyes popped open and he threw on his glasses. "I asked you for these last Tuesday."

She didn't respond as she walked over to the windowsill. She picked up the watering can and began to feed the plant Myers never failed to neglect.

He watched her as she lifted the watering can and doused the plants. She did this in a very deliberate and loving manner. He had seen her do it before and was always touched by how much attention she would give each of the four plants. She would lightly stroke their leaves and speak to them in Spanish.

He looked over her five-foot-eight frame from head to toe and saw she nearly peaked at six feet with the heels she wore. She wore a black skirt that was far too tight to be considered proper business attire and a white blouse that was about to burst. She had painted her nails a hot red, which was new, Myers noticed. Her hair was pulled up and held by a clip on the top of her head. Was she wearing glasses? He squinted his eyes. She was wearing fake eye glasses!

He cleared his throat. "How long are you going to be mad at me?"

"Mad?" she asked without taking her eyes off the plants. "Who's mad? It's a place of business, you said. Better we act as professionals."

Professionals, he thought, *now that's a laugh.* There was nothing professional about the entire operation. Not about her and not about the animal clinic as an establishment. She could barely file, her typing was a horror, and her phone manners ranged anywhere from near perfect to absolutely abysmal depending on her mood. To think she graduated from a secretarial school. She even had a certificate to prove it.

Myers knew the real reason for her uneven work ethic, too. It was beneath her; she didn't accept it.

Even the clients the clinic attracted were suspect. Most of them never actually paid Myers for his services with money. They paid him off in trade. Seeing as most of his clients were widowed Italian women in rent-controlled apartments and living off whatever savings accounts they had, they mostly paid him in meals. The best meals he ever tasted, but that's how they paid him. Myers could never say no to them because they were good to him and he actually liked them.

It drove Cynthia to tears to know that a grown man, a professional man, no less, ran his business this way.

Myers was very lucky to have a contract with the NYPD's canine division to keep his head barely above water.

He took a stab at standing up and sat back down twice as fast. "Cynthia," he said, "I'm thirty-three years old...you're what, twenty-two?"

"Three," she said.

"Huh?"

"Three. I'm twenty-three, and I'll be twenty-four in October."

"OK, fine. You're twenty-three and I'm thirty-three. Doesn't that seem a little odd to you?"

"No."

He caught a glimpse of himself in the mirror. He looked as bad as he felt. He could fit luggage in the bags under his eyes.

He liked her. He really liked her, but didn't like the way he felt around her, nervous and excited. His heart would beat so fast and heavy he'd think he was having a heart attack. Like when he would sit at his desk and she would stand next to him and look over his shoulder. From the corner of his eye, he could make out the curve of her breast or feel her hip lightly touch his arm, and everything about him would turn upside down. When she was around he could lose basic motor function, which also meant he could stutter, stammer, and become overtly spastic and red faced. On several occasions he did, and as a result, Myers figured he would be fine if he kept quiet and moved as little as possible when she was near.

She mistook this for him being a dick.

She finished watering the plants and put the watering can down. "Dr. Myers, I would appreciate it if during the course of business hours you keep the context of our conversations strictly professional." She tapped the eraser end of a pencil on her front tooth. "However, if you were to take me to dinner this evening at… oh, let's say some nice place on Mulberry Street, I'm sure we could come to some kind of agreement we can both benefit from."

Myers didn't know whether to laugh in her face or hug her. He appreciated her whole new way of talking and her attempt at dressing the part of someone who possessed even the slightest knowledge of professional conduct. He knew she was too smart to spend the rest of her life working as a receptionist in his animal clinic. That's what really scared him. He feared that if they did get involved she would eventually outgrow him. So Myers told himself that all Cynthia really had for him was a schoolgirl's passing crush. The problem was that she was stubborn. She was also tenacious, but he saw that she could get easily distracted and sidetracked.

He remembered when she first arrived at the animal clinic a little more than a year before; she was taking night classes at the Borough of Manhattan Community College. It didn't matter to Myers that she didn't actually have a major or that she hadn't even bothered to pick a path. Somewhere along the line, she lost interest in her classes and stopped going. She didn't have a boyfriend or a crew of girls that she would go partying with, either. All she wanted to do, it seemed, was work in the clinic. She was, however, very talented with handling the animals as they all just took to her. It didn't matter if it was cats, dogs, birds, reptiles, or even the rare tarantula; she had a knack with animals.

Now she's trying her hand at blackmail, Myers thought, *or at driving a hard bargain, at least.* Who was he fooling? He knew he was going to give in like he always did with her. The Puerto Rican lightning bolt melted him them as she had done the first time he saw her. He looked past her fake eyeglasses and into her velvet-black eyes. They were so warm.

He felt his own eyes lacked that warmth. His were an icy blue that went well with his sometimes stiff-as-a-board demeanor. His blonde hair showed the early signs of gray, but he was lucky enough to possess an appearance of not being older than twenty-seven.

"Cynthia," he started.

"Ms. Batista, if you don't mind."

He paused, bit his lip, and forced a smile. "If meeting you socially will get you to talk to me again, then so be it."

She nodded officiously. "Very good."

He opened the door for her. "Has anyone called?"

She actually had to think about it. "That little boy called about his frog. I told him he can pick it up later."

Myers noticed the change her mood had already taken. Her tone was upbeat and nearly perky. He could see the early stages of a smile that revealed her overbite.

She collected the brown paper bags from the box on his desk. "I'll leave these in the refrigerator."

After she left, he sat back down at his desk. He leaned back, put his feet up, and shut his eyes.

Myers had never thought of himself as a stiff until he had arrived in the neighborhood a little more than two years before. Suddenly he was surrounded by Catholics; what a culture shock! It was so different from his Midwest upbringing. Prior to setting foot on the island of Manhattan, his exposure to Catholics had been limited, and the ones he found himself living among were different from the few he had encountered before. In the immediate area there were some Irish, a few Puerto Ricans, but the overwhelming majority of the neighborhood was Italian. The parents were almost always from Italy and usually spoke English with a thick accent. The grandparents were always from the old country and spoke very little if any English. The Italian kids in the neighborhood were almost all American born and bilingual. In short, he knew little about Catholics and even less about Italians.

Naturally, he was leery of them at the start. However, after a few weeks Myers had forgotten all about his misconceptions about Italians from Hollywood movies. He even forgot about the luncheon meat he was raised on and learned that there was a lot more to pasta than just spaghetti. It was as if his taste buds held some vendetta against him as they exploded, screamed, and danced some heathen mambo in his mouth when he began to eat the food the locals made him. Were the sauces, the meats, and the hunks of cheese that they insisted on stuffing into his mouth actually supposed to taste that good? For the first few weeks of eating those dishes, Myers had a mouthful of canker sores.

To the locals, particularly the widows, Myers wasn't so much a stiff as he was an endearing dope that missed the point of everything. His clothes alone led them to believe this about him. Whoever chose his wardrobe, they'd say, must have had a good sense of humor.

So what if he wasn't Italian, wasn't Catholic, and didn't know how to dress? Who was perfect anyway? He was, they all agreed, a decent person and he had potential.

From outside the window there came a loud smacking sound. The handball soared through Myers's open window, bounced off his desk, whipped upward, and slammed right into his forehead. His eyeglasses exploded off his nose, and he fell backward, flailing his arms spastically. Finally, his chair gave out on him and he fell on his back.

The blue handball rolled to a stop by the trash can near his desk.

Outside, the radio went dead as the sounds of muffled laughter and whispers tickled his ears. On his back, he searched for his glasses. He gave up looking. Then he pulled himself to his feet and opened his desk drawer for his spare pair of glasses. He leaned over, picked up the handball, and gently tossed it back out the window.

A moment passed in silence.

"Thanks!" a young voice rang out. Within seconds the blaring radio came back on.

There was a knock at the door. Cynthia poked her head inside. "That police sergeant is here to pick up Comanche. Should I get him from upstairs in the kennel?"

Myers tapped his temple and his eye caught the bottle of whiskey in the trash can. "No. I'll do it. Tell him I'll be out in a minute."

As she stepped back, she stopped herself and did a double take. "You're wearing your backup glasses. Did something happen to the other pair?"

"No," he said. "I just felt like a change."

"Myers."

"Yes?"

She bit her bottom lip and smiled. "I'm really looking forward to tonight."

He waited to hear the door shut. Then he took the bottle out of the trash can and stuck it in the side drawer of his desk.

Chapter 3

Beyond a wall of glass in front of him, Baby Vines watched as Frank Balistrieri played Paganini's Fifth on a well-worn Fender Stratocaster. He had heard Frank play it a few times before, but was always amazed by Frank's interpretation. It was also during such moments that Vines was able to see Frank in a relaxed state. So much of the time, particularly lately, Frank was either anxious or nervous. He knew that Frank wasn't comfortable with all the attention he was getting lately. The pressure was on to produce, and the pressure to make tough decisions was on the horizon for Frank. This was the day before the night of their showcase for the A&R people at a club on Avenue A called The French Donut. Vines had been on the losing end of the music business for years, but through his experience he got to know a lot of people, and he invited all the right A&R people. He also knew a bidding war over Frank's band was about to take place.

He glanced at his watch and a flicked a light switch on the wall. The light flashed on and off in the cluttered rehearsal space beyond the glass. He watched Frank take off his guitar, place it on its stand, and turn off his amp. The studio door opened and Frank walked in. He gestured for Frank to take a seat.

Frank slid out the chair and sat down. He picked up the open pack of Algonquin-brand cigarettes from where it sat to the side of the mixing board and shook one out.

Frank didn't think Baby Vines looked like a record producer. He thought he looked like a bigger, black version of Mr. Clean. Vines was six foot five with a shaved head, hands as big as baseball mitts, and biceps the size of grapefruits. A gold loop dangled from his left earlobe. He wore a tight-fitting black T-shirt that stretched around his biceps like a second skin, and wore a pair of faded, snug Levis. He didn't look like the type of guy who spent too many hours in a darkened recording studio going over the same string of notes endlessly.

But that's exactly what he did do.

"A lot of my job is just what you see here. Me working the dials, barking orders at all of you, and making you do the same things over and over a billion times. That's my job and, I think you'd agree, I'm good at it. But that's only part of it. See, all the big names in this business, the people who actually make money, can sniff out a diamond mine. You see where I'm going with this?"

Frank nodded as his eyes strayed and slowly crawled up the sixteen-track mixing board next to Vines.

"There are a million schmucks just like me out there doing this. Now, I'm forty years old. Another few years and I'm too old to go around searching for a gig, hoping that the phone rings, and waiting on every flake in the business to give me a call. I'm done with that. Like all those other bozos, I've done my share of session work and every one of us is hoping to walk out of the jungle with a fifty-foot gorilla. The difference between them and me is I found the fifty-foot gorilla." He held up his hand. Between his index finger and thumb was a cassette tape labeled *Fly-Trap: Demo*. "This is pure gold, and every single one of those A&R flakes is getting a copy of this before the showcase."

"Seeing as I wrote it, you think that I can get a copy for myself?"

"Nice try." Vines shook his head and grinned. "Not yet. For the time being, it's the only copy. We need to talk about what's coming up because the offers you guys are going to get will make your head spin. Spend ten minutes with some of these A&R people and you'll feel like a Saudi prince the way they treat you." He ran his big hand over his face in exasperation. "This is all about you, Frank. The band, the showcase, all those A&R people tonight…it's all about you. It's important that you're in the right frame of mind. The point I'm trying to get across is that it's important you surround yourself with the right people."

"You're talking about Tommy," Frank said.

Vines nodded. "That's right; I am. I let him hear the demo earlier and he wasn't happy because he doesn't understand it. See, he's a good guy, and despite what he thinks, I like him, I really do. But he's the last one to show up and the first to leave. He's not very good on the bass—and before you chime in, he never will be. He's never going to be able to keep up with you and Moe. He just doesn't have it. I know Moe's been trying to teach him all kinds of things and trying to motivate him, but that you've carried him this far is a miracle. Can he learn his parts and get better? Sure. Will he? I doubt it. In this business, you need talent, a work ethic, and a lot of luck. Tommy's got luck for sure. But he's got very little talent and, God knows, zero work ethic. I'll be honest, his face alone could sell a million records in the right market, and that's the problem."

"Selling records is a problem?"

Vines shook his head. "The problem is these record-company suits can sniff out an easy million like a shark smells blood in the water. They always could, but now it's even worse since MTV took off. Tommy will become the focal point of the band because he'll look good in a magazine or on MTV, and the record company will water down your songs so they can reach the widest audience possible. Within two years you guys will be washed up, broke, and kicked to the curb like yesterday's newspaper and all your friendships will be destroyed."

Frank left the studio and stepped out into the heat on the sidewalk of Lafayette and Spring Streets. The heavy door slammed shut behind him. The scattered sunlight blinded him despite the gray and overcast sky. His eyes needed a few moments to adjust. As they did, he thought about what Vines had said about Tommy. He actually felt worse and emotionally drained. He just wanted to go home and take a nap.

Frank should have been happy; he knew that much. He was getting a shot that only one in a million ever got, and his life was about to change. No more living in rent-controlled walk-ups and having to feel privileged because of it; in a few years he could have a mansion, a Lamborghini, his picture on the cover of *Rolling Stone*, be called the Mozart of his time, and have a different starlet on his arm every week. In a few years he could actually buy the building he lived in.

Still, there was only one thing he wanted.

Since she dumped him, he hated this part of the day. Rehearsal was over and he had nowhere else to go. Even if Moe and Tommy were free, Frank didn't feel like playing handball and smoking weed behind Doc Myers's anymore. He didn't feel like being around those girls Moe and Tommy collected either.

He popped a cigarette in his mouth and fumbled in the front pocket of his jeans for a match. The air was so hot his pants clung to him like plastic wrap and his mane of black hair stuck to his face. He flipped a clump of it away from his line of vision, and as he did so he knew what he saw from the corner of his eye.

She stood by a parking meter just a few yards away.

Then she called his name.

What a mixture of emotions flooded him at that moment. Of all the days for her to show up, it had to be that one. He was nervous enough. He felt like shit and he knew he looked like it, too. When he looked at her it was like someone jabbed his heart with an ice pick.

Why did he look? If he had just kept his head down he could have walked away and…Who was he fooling? He was nuts to believe anything other than a void could ever grow between them. She was an old-money WASP—her family could be traced back to the earliest settlements in the New World. Frank, on the other hand, was a downtown Catholic, the son of immigrant parents. He never really knew his father because he died when Frank was only five. He was raised by his mother in a small rent-controlled railroad flat on Thompson Street in an otherwise predominately Italian neighborhood.

She fidgeted with her hands and stepped closer.

For nearly two minutes, they stared at each other in silence. Like two duelists about to square off, each one waited for the other to say something.

Frank knew it could all end at that moment if he could only turn and walk away. He couldn't take his eyes off her five-foot-six-inch frame, her hazel eyes, or her blonde hair that fell down her back and ended at a point.

"I want to talk," she said.

"Talk?"

She nodded.

"What for?"

Helplessly she looked away and half shrugged.

He watched and had to question what he witnessed. Was that really a lump growing in her throat, real tears welling up, or was it just it his imagination?

"What am I to you anyway, some walking dildo you fuck a few times when you're not out yachting with your girlfriends or doing whatever it is you people do?" The cigarette made him sick. He flicked it into the street.

"Is that what you really think?"

"I don't know what to think."

"Maybe I missed you."

"Maybe that's too bad." He looked her up and down. "Take care of yourself."

She made a side step to block him. "I don't have a lot of time."

"What, are you dying now?"

"Listen to me!" She clutched his wrist. "There's something I have to tell you, but not like this."

He reeled back.

"My mother's trying to take me to the Breakers tomorrow and..."

"The Breakers? I don't even know what that is."

"It's a resort...in Florida," she blurted as she shook her head. She crossed his lips with her index finger to keep him quiet. He smelled baby powder. "She's taking me down there for the rest of the summer and for who knows how long. I don't think I'm even going to take my classes in the fall. I don't know what's going to happen. I know you're mad and probably hate me right now and you have every right to but..."

"Yes?"

"Wait for me, Frank."

"Wait for you? You don't even know when you're coming back...if you're coming back."

She shook her head frantically and crossed his lips again. "Tonight. Wait for me by the 1 and 9 trains at King Street at ten o'clock and I'll be there."

"King Street?" Was she crazy? Then it hit him. "Oh, I get it. You're planning on running away. You really think your old man's going to let that happen? He'll have me arrested for kidnapping or something and I'll spend the next twenty years getting buttf—" He shivered at the thought. "Use your head, Amy. You're just stalling for time."

"No. I'm not." She kept her eyes locked onto his. "Will you?"

"Wait for you?"

"Yes."

He rubbed his chin to give the appearance that he actually thought it over. "I'd say I'm not the sharpest knife in the drawer, but I'm not that dumb. Thanks, but no."

He walked away and wished he had another cigarette, his heart beat so hard. She called him again.

She stood with her arms spread apart. "What do I have to do, you temperamental prick?" She spotted an empty beer bottle off the curb. She squatted, picked it up, and with the skill of a seasoned street fighter, cracked it in half. "You want me to bleed for you?" She pressed the jagged edge against the inside of her wrist.

He rolled his eyes. "Put the bottle down, Amy. I've had enough drama in my life lately." Gently he took the bottle from her hand and flipped it off into the street. "You know, the old loons around here used to tell us to never go west of Sixth Avenue at night."

She smirked. "So does that mean you'll be there?"

"Yes," he answered.

She had him then as she always did. Words from a Bruce Springsteen song came back to haunt him, something about it not being easy to break him, but that she could and would find a way.

She took his hand and squeezed it. "Ten o'clock. Meet me at King Street at ten o'clock."

Chapter 4

Al Lucchese looked across the desk at Charlie DeMarco's perfectly round bald head and thought that, barring DeMarco's thin black mustache, he resembled a meatball. Charlie DeMarco wasn't a contract killer, but a small, low-level wise guy that ran a numbers racket out of a candy store on the corner of Sullivan Street right across the street from St. Anthony's Church. DeMarco did, however, provide a specific disposal service on occasion for some of the bigger fish of the area's criminal element. DeMarco was a middleman who rarely got his hands dirty.

They were seated at a folding card table in the store's basement, which had a dusty floor, but was broom clean and well lit. Cardboard boxes were lined in rows along the walls and stacked on top of each other in such a way that gave the basement a cozy but slightly claustrophobic feel. On the plus side, the basement was somewhat dank, but the air was naturally cool and that made all the difference on such a hot day.

Lucchese was a hard-looking man, what the old-timers would have called a head breaker, which is why DeMarco kept him around. By the time he was eighteen he had been involved in over a hundred street fights and earned the nickname the Bulldog of Canal Street. His knuckles wore the scars of the hits he gave while his face wore the marks of the hits he took and his body wore the scars and cuts from the stabs and blows he took. In a nutshell, Lucchese gave as good as he got.

By the time his tour in Korea ended in 1952 he had already been awarded the Bronze Star for heroism at the Chosin Reservoir. As a cop he had more collars and more commendations than anyone else in his precinct.

"You're, ah, probably wondering why I called you here," Charlie DeMarco said with a clap of his pudgy hands and a short-lived smile that dropped the second his twenty-nine-year-old nephew Ronnie brought him his morning coffee. DeMarco looked up. "Where's his?" he asked with a gesture toward Lucchese.

Lucchese saw that Ronnie wasn't fazed, but was annoyed with his uncle's question. "Where's whose what?"

DeMarco clamped his eyes shut and winced as if Ronnie's question had caused him actual physical pain.

"*Spoiled brat,*" Lucchese heard whispered in his ear. He knew it was the priest and smirked. "*Pussy aristocrat is what he is. It's only a matter of time until you're taking orders from this fuckin' idiot. Hell of a life you've carved out for yourself.*"

"Fuck off." Lucchese sneered. It was a love-hate relationship with the priest. He could be very funny and a real pal, but on a dime the priest would turn into a nasty asshole.

"*What, like you're surprised? Jesus Christ, how on earth did you not see this coming?*"

Lucchese mumbled something nasty beneath his breath.

"*Don't be mad at me. I wanted you to get as far away from here as possible. I wanted you to be happy.*"

DeMarco and his nephew continued to talk, but Lucchese didn't hear any of it because the priest's face appeared in the wisps of smoke from the tip of Ronnie's cigarette. One minute Lucchese watched as DeMarco and Ronnie got into it, but when he looked back there he was. He stood right behind DeMarco, dressed in his white collar with black shirt, black pants, and black rubber-soled shoes. He was a lean man of about sixty who stood six feet tall with a ring of white hair that wrapped his head in a horseshoe. The top of his head was a bald dome. Gin blossoms spread out on his cheeks like red branches of lightning.

"*He really does look like a meatball, doesn't he?*" the priest asked Lucchese as he lifted a cigarette out DeMarco's open pack on the table. He leaned in and sniffed. "*Come here. You're not going to believe this, but he actually smells like salami and provolone.*"

Lucchese looked away to stifle his laugh. Seeing this only encouraged the priest to make silly faces behind DeMarco's back. Lucchese had to look away again, but when his eyes came back DeMarco was talking to him again.

"Yes or no?"

"What?" Lucchese said.

"Do you want coffee?"

"No."

DeMarco turned to Ronnie. "Now, was that so hard?" He made a dismissive gesture with a flap of his hand. "So, you're probably wondering why I wanted to see you."

Lucchese nodded.

"We've got a problem…"

"Which is?"

DeMarco pursed his lips as he locked his stare into Lucchese's eyes for a full ten seconds. "I never did understand how you came up with that place, but I'm glad you did," he said with a laugh and then stopped abruptly so that his face became stone. "Here's the problem, Bettancourt bought the place."

Lucchese's hands constricted into tight fists.

"It's a tragedy really," DeMarco added. "He paid the city all the back taxes and they gave it to him for next to nothing. As we speak, he's already got a construction crew setting up the staging area, and they break ground tomorrow morning. Well, it was good while it lasted, but this means we're going to have to relocate some of the…ah…debris."

CHAPTER 5

She's not coming, a voice in the back of Frank's mind said. Somehow he knew all along that she wouldn't, no matter how much he wanted to believe otherwise. Amy Van Tassel, actress, dancer, and amateur photographer, was starting Juilliard in the fall. It hurt like hell. She could do that to him.

An hour and three cigarettes later, he looked like a wet rat and felt like a fool in the rain. He stood right where she said she would meet him, on the corner of Varick and King. His back pressed against the dingy brick wall of a bodega that had been abandoned a long time ago. A tiny sliver of awning still remained but did little to keep the elements at bay. His hair was a matted mess from the rain, his sweat, and the humidity. He stood with his hands stuffed into his front pockets, feeling like the world's biggest sap.

The subway rumbled beneath him. The muffled brakes screeched as a train pulled into the station. Down below, the train let out a long hiss, then took off, chugging to the next station. He waited, hoping against hope that she would come up those steps. She didn't. No one did. Just like the three previous trains.

The rain turned to an annoying but light drizzle. He raised his face to the sky and looked at the gray and bloated clouds that had hovered over the city all summer. He didn't care if it started to rain again. He had no place in mind, but knew he couldn't go back to his empty apartment on Thompson Street.

With a labored sigh he headed west with nowhere in mind despite the heat and the heavy, muggy skank feeling in the air. It was after hours in the printing district. The place was a ghost town after five o'clock. The only sign of life that existed during the day was the heavy reek of printer's ink. When he reached Hudson Street, he took a right turn and cut across the empty street.

He wasn't paying attention. His head hung low as he walked, puffing on another cigarette. He heard a tiny, metallic jangling.

Something clipped his shoulder. His left ankle gave out. His legs stuttered. He did a half spin and hit the sidewalk face-first.

He lay with his cheek pressed to the wet, filthy sidewalk. His palm and jaw hurt like hell. His eyes popped open. A woman's foot, set in a high heel, stood before him.

CHAPTER 6

"**I** wasn't paying attention," a woman's voice confessed in an accent Frank couldn't put his finger on. "I didn't see you coming around the corner and…"

Frank looked up, rubbing the sore spot on his hand. She was a slender woman in a sleeveless shirt and a skirt that fell just below her knees. Metal bangle bracelets hung in lopsided clusters around her wrists.

"Your hand," she said, squatting so they were face-to-face. She had thick, dark-brown hair, a brown so deep it bordered on black. Her long, wavy mane fell down to her defined arms and stopped just above her elbows. A silver arm bracelet fit snugly around her left bicep.

She could have been Southern European or possibly Persian or Arab. He couldn't be sure, but there was a definite Mediterranean air to her.

The bangles jingled as she gently took hold of his wrist. Her fingertip zigzagged down his palm. He winced when she touched the soft spot.

"That hurts?" she asked as she moved her finger away.

He felt like such a clown—out of place, insecure, helpless, and anxious.

"I didn't break it, did I?" Her fingertips touched her lips. He noticed her fingernails. They were a half inch long, unpolished, and well manicured.

"No." He forced a weak smile. "It's fine." He avoided her eyes but kept his hand in hers.

The expression on her face changed to one of concern. She touched his cheek. "You're bleeding." She turned her hand so the tip of her finger faced him.

He watched the crimson drop slide down her slender finger. "I think I broke your lip."

He touched the spot, smiled for a moment, and let out a nervous laugh. "It's a fat lip. It's nothing really..." He looked at her from the corners of his eyes, his head low, shoulders hunched.

"I'm sure I have something for that upstairs." Her eyes widened, and despite the darkness, they glowed a deep and lush green. "I'd hate for this to get infected."

She caressed his chin with her fingertips, turning his face toward her own, and his heart nearly exploded.

Now he had to look at her.

Her green eyes gleamed. The corner of her mouth curled into a smirk. "Come. I'll take care of that for you." She took hold of his wrists and guided him to his feet. She straightened the short sleeves of his black T-shirt. "I only live right over there."

Shyly, he rubbed the back of his neck. "Really, I'm fine. You don't have to—"

"I insist." She took his hands again. "I won't be able to sleep tonight unless I know that you are well."

Chapter 7

"**W**atch as you go," her voice called from the darkness. "There's a hole in the ground and I'd hate for you to trip."

She led him by his right hand under a high, arched brick entrance. It was to the side of an abandoned warehouse or foundry or some other industrial-type building. Frank had seen it his whole life and heard the stories about it, but he'd never actually been this close. Like much of the area, the building was abandoned. Frank was glad he'd listened to her. God forbid he left her alone and she got raped or worse. He thought it was strange that she lived on that side of the neighborhood. Frank knew about the people claiming to be artists that lived around there, but not in that building.

The arched side entrance was more like a pitch-black tunnel. The distance they walked seemed endless. He felt like he should have a torch. They finally came out of the black tunnel and into a dimly lit courtyard in the rear of the building. She led him up a short flight of metal steps and onto a loading dock where she opened a heavy steel door. It gave with a stutter, revealing a gaping void within.

"I've only just moved in," she said, standing at the threshold. "The lights aren't all working, I'm afraid. Let me go up first and open the upstairs for you so you can see a little on your way up."

Frank nodded, but felt uneasy. He watched as her body sank into the darkness. He looked back and saw the clumpy, shadowy shapes of construction equipment that cluttered the courtyard. A four ton-sized Dumpster sat against the wall of the loading dock. In the dim light, he could make out some lettering of the name of the company that owned it.

He heard the sound of a door opening and saw her standing above him on a landing, washed in a wobbling and throbbing white light. He carefully climbed the lopsided set of worn, wooden steps.

As he reached the landing, she stood with her back to the open door. With a wave of her hand, she gestured for him to enter. Like a stray cat, he passed through the threshold and found himself in an enormous loft space. The gap between the floor and the ceiling was immense. The wobbling light, he discovered, came from several small candles positioned around the room, casting dancing shadows that pulsated and throbbed on the hardwood floor and walls.

He heard the door slowly close with a whine.

She took his hand and, with a trot, led him deeper into the space. She opened a small door to a washroom. A tea candle flickered on the small white sink.

"There's a towel to the right of the sink," she said.

He lowered his head and thanked her through his wet, straggly locks. He closed the door, turned on the faucet, cupped his hands, and splashed cold water on his face. It felt good. He ran a wet hand on the back of his neck, rolled his head back, and wet his throat. He dried his hands and face. When he looked forward, he was surprised there was no mirror on the wall; just the outline where one had once been.

Thunder growled in the sky.

Frank patted his face with the towel. As he stepped out of the bathroom, his eyes widened with amazement by the amount of light that now filled the loft. Yellowish with an accent of orange, the light from candles at all points in the loft flickered, throbbed, pulsated, and massaged everything within. For the first time, he had a real look at the place.

His first impression was correct: the space was immense. The open room stretched from one end of the building to the other. He counted seven multipaned windows facing Van Dam Street. Within the loft was an elaborate display of antiques, ornate furniture, and area rugs. Candles flickered along walls decorated with sconces.

He looked for the woman but didn't see her anywhere.

The boards in the hardwood floor creaked beneath the soles of his Pro-Keds. He noticed a large, black couch in the center of the floor. Its four legs flared up and out, then at their midsections, went back inward. It made Frank think of a giant and still spider perched on top of a wooden bannister. Above the couch was a skylight. The black rectangle flashed a bright white for a sliver of a second. A few seconds later, more thunder rolled in the sky.

Somewhere in the loft, a clock was ticking.

Frank's eyes tried to follow his ears and locate it, but his attention was side-tracked when he noticed a wall lined with books at the far end of the loft. It seemed that with each new glance, more contents of the loft revealed themselves to him like a wreck coming into view in pieces and sections to a scuba diver. The books, all leather-bound hardcover editions, were neatly arranged from floor to ceiling. A ladder on a track rested at the far right of the wall near the last of the seven windows.

Then his eye caught a lumpy shape on the floor, masked by the shadows. Frank stepped closer for a better look and saw that it was a life-size figure of a person in a crouched position, arms crossing its chest with hands that reached for something not there. At the figure's base, Frank noticed the crumbled remains of what looked to be plaster. The odd statue was brittle looking and chalky white. Its mouth was stretched open wide and its eyes were two black, depthless sockets.

Frank saw other traces of powdery flakes on the floor. His eyes followed the trail, spying several more of these plaster statues. As his eyes wandered further to a darkened corner in the space, adjusting to the light, he was able to make out the impression of a mound made of plaster statues that rose twelve feet high.

As if a slight whisper blew in his ear, his attention was stolen again. He shifted his view away from the books and saw a rectangular box roughly seven feet high and four and a half feet wide that loomed like an ancient monolith or immovable boulder. Its lower half was solid wood, but the upper half was glass on all sides with a wood crown on top of it. Within the box, Frank saw the torso, head, and arms of the man inside it.

He angled past the spiderlike couch, stepping closer until he could see green lettering painted on the black crown. In a font Frank had only seen in carnivals and bazaars was written, *The Hierophant*.

Just above the man's lower half, on the outside of the box, was a coin slot. Frank had seen boxes similar to this every June at the Feast of St. Anthony or at the San Gennaro Festival every September. But he had never seen one quite like this before him. Normally they were populated with some gaudy-looking gypsy woman with a crystal ball or some oddball kook in a turban with a loud emerald in the center of his forehead. This box was as different as the man inside. The character within looked so real, Frank actually thought it was a live person. The man looked to be in his late fifties with black hair peppered and aged appropriately with gray spots. He had a matching goatee and thin wire-rimmed glasses and was dressed in a black three-piece suit. As he stepped closer, Frank saw that the man's right arm was raised and in his hand was a crudely carved wooden stake. In the man's other hand, down by his side, was a wooden mallet.

The man's eyes gave Frank a funereal chill. They seemed to hold some dimming or pleading light behind them. The frozen and fear-stricken pose of the man in the box coupled with those eyes made Frank uneasy.

He jumped as something touched his ankle. He looked down, felt it again, and saw a small black cat at his feet. It rubbed against his ankle, turned quickly, and did the same with the other side. He reached down and touched the cat's smooth, velvet-like head. The cat looked at Frank with its glowing emerald eyes and sprinted off into the shadows and darkness.

That elusive clock still ticked.

He stood up, wondering where the cat went. For just a moment, a silly idea skipped across his mind. The woman was nowhere to be seen, so...

He shook his head and shook off the stupid thought. The cat and the woman were not one and the same. He turned and looked at the man in the box again.

He jumped back when he saw her face through the far side of the glass.

He felt like an idiot and hoped she hadn't seen his overreaction. He felt awkward and thought he had been a little too comfortable to walk over to the box in the first place.

"I'm sorry," he said. "I just saw this from over there and—"

"And what?" she asked.

CHAPTER 8

"For a minute," Frank said as he took a long and hard look at the man in the box, "I thought he was real. Where did you get this?"

Her mouth stretched into a noncommittal smile.

Something in that man's wide and awestruck eyes caused the hairs on his neck to rise. Yet it was the demoralized expression beneath the surface that made Frank's heart sink. The more he stared at it, the worse he felt.

The tips of his fingers lightly grazed the coin slot. "If I slipped a coin in here, would he tell me my fortune?" he asked. "Is that what he's supposed to do?"

She shook her head. "I'm sorry, but he's broken. He has been for some time now. However, in his day he was quite the soothsayer." She noticed Frank's confused expression. "Fortune teller."

It was as if a lightbulb went off over his head. She was an artist, this was her loft, and The Hierophant was a piece she created. "It's really very good. It's very real looking. How did you do it?"

She smirked. "It's all smoke and mirrors." She waved her hand. "Besides, a good magician never reveals her secret."

"That's too bad," he said, taking a long last look at it. "I guess I should get going..." He trailed off as she rounded the box and stepped before him. She was older; that much he knew, but he couldn't pinpoint her age. He assumed she was somewhere in her mid-thirties, but it was almost impossible to be sure. She possessed a charm, however, that made her age, whatever it may be, irrelevant.

"Stay," she said. Her face was within inches of his. "Stay for one drink."

He looked down and saw that she held a half-filled glass of wine in each hand. He took the glass she extended to him and felt her fingertips gently caress his hand.

"Sit." She placed her hand on his lower back and gently guided him to the couch.

He walked ahead and sat on the seat's edge. As she crossed him to take her seat, he felt like a young girl out on a date with a man she hardly knew. She sat down at an ambiguous distance to his right. She crossed her right leg over her left knee and propped her arm on the back of the couch. Her arm was bent at the elbow so that she was able to twirl a strand of her hair.

Her right foot caught his eye as it dangled so close to his knee. He noticed a silver ring slipped around her middle toe.

"How is your hand...I don't even know your name," she said, looking up as she sipped from her glass.

"Frank," he said. "It's fine. I mean, my name is Frank and my hand is fine. It's feeling better."

"Short for something? Possibly Francis, Franco, Francisco, no?"

"Just Frank."

"And do you have a last name, Just Frank?"

He smiled. "Balistrieri."

"Balistrieri." She rolled the word deliciously over her tongue. "Italian?"

"Around here, who isn't?"

"What part of Italy are you from?"

"I was born here in New York. Right up Seventh Avenue in St. Vincent's. My parents were from there."

"Were?"

"They're both dead now. My father died when I was five and my mother died in January."

"I'm sorry to hear that." With a sigh, she settled herself more comfortably on the couch. Her foot bobbed up and down gently. "And what do you do, Frank?" she asked as the strand of hair slithered between her slow, twirling fingers.

He was paralyzed by her question. How to answer it? *The truth?* he wondered. *Sure, go ahead; tell her how you spend all your free time these days. Tell her how you brood and moan over some girl that left you in a lurch more times than you can remember, Frank. That is if you want to make her laugh.* "You mean for fun or, like, work or what?" *What am I, twelve?*

"For whatever."

He rubbed his neck. "I'm a musician…sort of."

"Sort of?"

"I mean, I am a musician, but…"

"Yes?"

Why couldn't he just say it? Why couldn't he just tell her that he was a musician on the verge of a record deal and that all the write-ups his band had gotten said he was the next guitar god? He could hear Moe's voice urging him, *"You have the newspaper write-up folded up in your wallet, baby. Show it to her, Frank. It's not bragging and it's not showing off."*

"I don't know." He sounded agitated, but it was really frustration with himself. He felt like an ass.

"You obviously play an instrument," she said, helping him along. "Which one or which ones?"

"I can play a few things, but…"

"Can you play that?" Her finger pointed past him.

He turned his head and with a strained face saw a grand piano standing near the man in the box. It was bathed in a soft white light from some unseen source above. How had he missed seeing it earlier?

"It's not really my forte, but yes, I can play it."

"Then come!" She jumped from the couch and took his hand.

With her hand draped behind her, she held on to his, leading him to the piano. He took a seat on the bench she had slid out for him.

"Is it tuned?" he asked.

"See for yourself."

His fingers touched the keys. The sound was perfect. "What should I play?"

She stood behind him, looking over his shoulder. "Something all your own."

She purred as she placed her hands on his shoulders. "No Beethoven, no Bach, no Chopin, or any other dead person's work. Something you've composed."

He plunged in.

She found her way back to the couch and laid herself out on it. Emotionally, the piece was a room of smoke and mirrors, but she could see through them. He shut his eyes and saw an entire story unfold in his mind. It was a story of suspicion, of a fear of being exposed, a distrust of others, and above all, the inability to distinguish one's friends from enemies. More than anything else it was about loneliness and longing.

CHAPTER 9

"*You're listening to 95.5 FM WPLJ. I'm Carol Miller and we're about halfway through a commercial-free hour...*"

The radio faded from Tommy's ears as he stepped out the front door and lit a cigarette. He leaned against the storefront glass beneath the pizzeria's red awning in the heat. For the most part, he wore the same thing he had earlier in the day with the exception of the Van Halen T-shirt. Instead, beneath his sauce-stained apron, he wore a red T-shirt that said *Vinny's Pizzeria* in wavy white letters. He had on the same pair of jeans and the same sneakers he wore earlier. It had been a slow night.

Tommy took advantage of it being slow by stacking all the bins with dough and filling up the vats with sauce for when Vinny Jr. arrived in the morning. He even filled those twenty jars with his sauce and labeled them with the stickers Vinny Sr. insisted on. It was a round white sticker with big red and rounded letters that said *Vinny's Own*, but it wasn't Vinny's; it was Tommy's sauce. Vinny said the jars of sauce were for him to take home and give to his family.

He looked across the street to a small café on the northeast corner where Bleecker crossed MacDougal Street. Café Borgia II it was called. He could see the usual burst of personality at the cash register. Some heavyset girl with wild brown hair like steel wool, no makeup, and no sense of humor. He had known her since grade school, and in all those years, she never so much as smiled at him. The thought of her naked turned him off to mayonnaise.

Even the foot traffic was extra light on Bleecker Street that night. A person here and there running to wherever to meet whoever, and only a few people had stepped in for a slice the whole night. None of the regular stragglers or characters had come by either.

A gold-colored Chevrolet IROC Camaro pulled up and stopped in front of the café across the street blocking the fire hydrant. The driver's-side door opened and out stepped Nicky Napoli. He had a stocky build and peaked at five eight. Even from the across the street, Tommy had to squint from the glare that Nicky's pinky ring gave off. A thick gold rope chain hung from his neck and from it swayed an equally heavy gold Christ head. Tommy rolled his eyes.

And then his heart sank.

He watched Anne-Marie Mariani step out of the passenger-side door. Tommy made a bitter face as he watched them walk into the café arm in arm.

"You know, Tommy," he heard Moe's voice echo in head, *"you're never going to get to smoke that bowl with Keith Richards working in a dump like Vinny's the rest of your life. You should learn those bass lines, bro."*

Smoking weed with Keith Richards, the rest of his life and anywhere else, seemed like a million miles away. He pulled his last drag off the cigarette and flicked it as far across the street as it would fly. It fell short of the IROC's front tire and sizzled out on the wet blacktop. He frowned and went back inside.

It was that time of night when all Tommy really had to do was count down the minutes until he could close the place. He leaned on the counter and read a copy of the evening edition of the *Post* that had been left behind by one of the night's few customers. He flipped over the front cover, followed his finger as it ran down the page to the table of contents. He licked his fingers and finally found the comics.

If he had turned the page he would have seen a small paragraph beneath the heading *Great-Granddaughter of Steel Magnate Missing* with a postage-stamp-sized photo of Amy Van Tassel.

When Tommy finished reading *Peanuts*, he looked at the clock on the wall, let out a sigh, walked to the back of the pizzeria, and turned off the overhead fluorescent lights and the neon sign in the window. He locked the door and then lowered the front gates. As he fastened the lock shut he noticed the gold IROC was gone.

He walked east to Thompson Street and then headed south. He crossed Houston Street, and as he neared the corner at Prince Street, something on the other side of the blacktop caught his eye. It was Anne-Marie Mariani's dainty and petite frame as it wiggled its way into the deli on the corner diagonally from him. She held the curved handle of a closed umbrella in her hand.

Tommy suddenly craved something sweet.

He stepped off the curb, waited for a cab to pass, and then crossed the blacktop to the deli. The deli's front door was open wide, and the air conditioner that hung above it was off. On the counter, a fan moved back and forth blowing hot air. Tommy walked straight back to the refrigerators at the far end of the store. He spotted her reflection in a round mirror up in the corner of the back wall as she reached into a glass refrigerator to grab a can of diet soda.

She had a long face and a sharp nose that matched her chin. Her hair, like every other Italian girl's in the neighborhood, was dark brown and long. The layers in her hair were starting to grow out, and Tommy liked the way it looked. She had squeezed herself into a pair of Sergio Valente jeans, a purple tube top, and a pair of hot-red Candie's heels. Her nails, fingers, and toes were painted to match her shoes. A thin gold bracelet dangled from her left wrist. Around her neck was a gold chain, and connected to the chain was an ankle bracelet that read, *Nicky and Anne-Marie.*

Tommy eyed the ankle bracelet. "What's with the dog tag, Anne?"

"What's it to you?" she said as she sidestepped him on her way back up the aisle.

"I don't know…I'm just thinking…"

She cocked an eyebrow. "Thinking?"

She placed the can of diet soda on the counter and took a cherry-flavored lollipop from a bucket to the side of the cash register.

"Wondering. I'm just wondering is all. Twos go with twos and nines go with nines. You and Nicky…c'mon…he looks like a bat, Anne." Tommy gestured to the kid behind the counter that he was paying her bill. He dropped a dollar on the counter. "And he's from Brooklyn."

"So?"

"So he drives an IROC."

"So?"

"We all know what IROC stands for. Besides, I thought you were smart. Didn't you get a scholarship to that college up the block?"

"A partial scholarship and it's called NYU. You could've gotten in if you applied yourself."

She ran her tongue along her top front teeth as her eyes took a long, slow walk up and down him. He beamed as she did this.

She peeled off the lollipop's wrapper and wrapped her red lips around it. Tommy began to melt.

"What color is the sock you have stuffed down your pants, Tommy?"

Sock? He mouthed the word. Then he realized where her eyes were focused. "You got it all wrong, Anne. See, I got no hips and I don't have much of an ass, so my pants, when they fall, hang on to the one thing that's there."

She eyed his hips and saw there was some truth to what he said, but she had heard the rumors of what Tommy had swinging between his legs. She couldn't tell if he was being coy or sincere. "Do you have a tapeworm or something? You never seem to gain weight and you eat everything."

"Oh, no, it's just that I'm a growing boy and my metabolism is pretty good. At least that's what Dr. Januzzi said. Well, that's not really true. I don't have a much of an appetite lately."

"Why's that?" She crinkled her forehead and clicked her tongue.

"I got this aching heart and…" He had to look away to hide the strained expression on his face.

"Tommy Santalesa, you are so full of shit it's not even funny!" Her face exploded into a beaming smile. "The closest you ever came to a broken heart is when you broke mine in the eighth grade playing spin the bottle with Nadine Katsukawa at Angelo Ranieri's confirmation party." She scoffed and laughed as she stepped out of the store onto the sidewalk.

"You're still holding that against me? That was years ago, and besides, she seduced me."

"She was thirteen…"

"Those Japanese women can be very persuasive."

"...and only half Japanese. Her mother was Portuguese."

He crossed in front of her and stopped with his hands on his hips. "What? What did I do now?"

"Oh, please!" She swatted her hand, and her bracelet jingled as she did this. She stepped closer to him, and with her fingernail, she flipped out the pack of cigarettes he kept pressed between the top button of his jeans and his flat stomach. "As if you've ever had such an emotion in your life."

"No, I'm serious, Anne-Marie. " He placed a hand over his heart while, with his other hand, he cracked open the lid of his lighter for her cigarette. "Swear to God I am. What do you want me to do, not say anything?"

Dragging on her cigarette, she pulled a frown. "Tommy, you just like my lipstick."

He shrugged. "I bet that'd be enough if it was Frank talking."

"Like, duh." She turned away from him and then turned up her nose. "He's not a sleaze." She turned and poked his stomach with the tip of her fingernail. "Unlike some people I know."

His eyes widened then moved up and away as his mouth grew into a guilty smile. "C'mon, Anne, give a fellow guinea a—"

"I don't like that word."

"Alright, alright." He stepped back and made a peace offering by showing her the palms of his hands. His hand then fell back to cover his heart and he hunched down somewhat so that he appeared to be on bended knee. "Give a guy..." He shook his head and made an expression of pain and redemption that was so fake it could have been a store-bought plastic mask. "No, Anne-Marie, give me a break."

Something bubbled within her that came out of her mouth and sounded like a frothing cappuccino machine. She covered her mouth as she giggled.

When she realized that his stupid expression and big brown puppy eyes weren't going anywhere, she stepped forward and placed her finger underneath his chin. "*Faccia brutta!*" she exclaimed as she squeezed his face.

He kept that position and expression for some time. Then he said, "Aw, c'mon, Anne-Marie, I've made it to the top of the big mountain of love and, God as my witness, I'm falling."

"Ha!" She covered her mouth and turned on her red-leather Candie's. She slowly strutted away.

Tommy didn't move at first. He enjoyed the sight too much as it swayed from left to right and then back again. His eyes followed her swaying like a hypnotist's swinging pocket watch and he nearly forgot his own name.

He sprang up and followed. Catching up to her, he touched her shoulder and stepped in front of her.

She feigned a scowl and then looked away for a moment. She liked it, and what girl wouldn't? He was gorgeous, but Anne-Marie knew what would happen if she gave in. Tommy had a big mouth, and the minute they were done he would be zipping up his pants, be out the door and over in the handball court telling everyone what had happened. Not because he was mean, or even sleazy, but just because he was Tommy.

"Look, let me tell you my situation here."

She rolled her eyes and did a quick once-over on her fingernails.

"What am I supposed to do? You look so…good in those jeans and those heels." He nearly bit the fat of his palm, but his eyes quickly found their way to his favorite spot, her chest. "And that tube top you're wearing is singing love songs to me like you don't know."

She scowled.

He jumped back. "Just bear with me for a minute here."

"Uh-huh." She stuck her palm out and felt a raindrop.

Tommy took the umbrella from her hand, opened it, and held it over both of them.

"So, there I am one night just sitting in front of my TV, eating a bowl of cereal and watching my favorite movie, *The Fish That Saved Pittsburgh*. I felt this breeze coming in from somewhere, but I didn't pay it any mind. Now, I must've heard something because I looked up and there's this little naked flying baby with white fluffy wings sticking out his back. He was just hovering up near the ceiling. So I jumped up and I'm like, 'Whoa, little-flying-naked-baby, be careful up there.' But he's not paying me any mind, so I try to catch him because I don't want him to hurt himself. As you know I tend to think of others a lot, being a good Catholic and all." He cleared his throat. "So I'm calling out to him—"

"Is there a point?" She sighed.

"Now, now, just bear with me a minute or two longer. So, I'm trying to catch him but I can't, so I slump back on the couch and then he looks at me and smiles. So I smile back figuring it'll make him more at ease. So I say, 'Hey, little-naked-flying-baby, why don't you come down here and watch TV with me?' He's flapping his wings and he starts to come down a little closer. So I stand up to catch him, but he pulls out a bow and aims an arrow at me. I'm like, 'No, little-flying-naked-baby, no!' But he doesn't listen. He pulls his arm back and lets the arrow fly. Hits me right here." Tommy touched his chest. "Bull's-eye. Next thing you know I'm on my back with an arrow sticking out my chest. He laughs in my face, the little creep, and flies back out the window. I look down at the arrow and what's written on it?"

"Wait, let me guess."

"It says Anne-Marie on it."

"Maybe it's another Anne-Marie; it's a pretty common name."

"No, it had your last name on it, too." He nervously rubbed his stomach, looking anywhere but at her. "That's what it said. Yeah."

She rubbed her chin and let out a sigh. "Did it say my confirmation name, too?"

What a zinger she just threw at him. "No, I don't think it did."

She rolled her tongue against her cheek and tapped her fingers on her left hip. "So, where's the arrow now?"

"Where is it now? I keep it under my pillow at home…in my bedroom…on my bed. Get what I'm saying?"

"Oh, yeah, Tommy, I get it. Sure."

He placed his hands on her shoulders and stepped closer. He stared into her eyes for a moment and then spoke in a low and soft voice. "So, look, I'm thinking since my sister Lisa's probably still at one of her booyah man-hater meetings tonight, we should go back to my place."

"Gee, I don't know, Tommy. I mean, I'd hate for you to think I'm like one of those skanks in your fan club."

"Fan club?"

"You know all those girls from St. Michaels that tramp it up by hiking up their uniform skirts and unbuttoning just about all the buttons on their blouses. You know, the ones that flock around the pizzeria every afternoon when you're working there."

"Oh, yeah, those girls." His smile lit up the street. Then he snapped out it. "You're not like them, Anne. That's why I like you."

Her tongue rolled around along the inside of her cheek. "You're going to show me that arrow?"

He shrugged. "Or something just as long."

CHAPTER 10

"Or something like that." Frank stared at his hands. He was emotionally drained, but he also felt purged, as if some toxin had been sweated out of him. He'd played that very same piece a hundred times before—always on his Stratocaster—but having heard it on piano was an altogether different experience with a different meaning. He had never played a piano that well in his life.

Aware that the piece was finished, she opened her eyes and she sprang to her feet. "Beautiful!" she cried as she rounded the couch. "And what do you call it?"

His mouth curled into a tight and embarrassed smile. He shook his head. "I'm not sure. I don't have a name for it yet."

"Tragic," she said, mulling it over. "Every great piece deserves a title." Her eyes scanned the loft as if the words were floating around waiting to be caught. "'An Act of Contrition.'"

He thought it over. "That's some title," he said.

Her eyes beamed directly into his, and for the first time that night, Frank did not shy away.

The skylight became a rectangle of bright white light again. It flickered and flashed for a moment, and then the pitter-patter of raindrops danced on the glass. It quickly escalated into a loud downpour.

"Sit here," she said, sliding her fingers along the back of the couch.

"Really," he said. "I should get going."

"Go where?" She laughed. "Look how it's raining."

Frank saw water splash against the multipaned windows as if it had been thrown from buckets.

"You're worried about imposing," she said, letting out a mocking chuckle. "As if you could ever lay such an offense before me. Nonsense." She stepped closer to him, placed her hands on his shoulders, and affectionately squeezed them. "So quick to assume. Tsk, tsk. If you only knew. Your mother would be proud knowing she raised such a well-mannered and considerate son. I suspect, however, there is more to it. You are, let's say…self-effacing?"

Frank agreed with a nod of his head. Strange, he thought, how she already understood that much about him.

They took their seats on the couch again. She assumed her earlier position, but sat closer to him. "If the piano isn't your forte, then what is?" She sipped from her glass.

"Mostly the guitar, but I've always had a knack with string instruments."

Her eyes widened enthusiastically. "And tell me, what does your girlfriend think of your music?"

His heart sank at the thought of Amy. Was she even his girlfriend anymore? Had she ever really been? "What makes you think I have girlfriend?" he said. It was impossible to look her in the eye.

"Oh, now you're just teasing me. A nice-looking young man such as yourself and you expect me to believe that you don't have a girlfriend? Ha! I'm flattered, but despite my youthful appearance, I wasn't born yesterday."

His cheeks flushed and he cracked a crooked smile. Feeling pressed, he ran his fingers through his hair. "Truth? The truth is I don't know what I have at the moment. Or what I ever did have."

She straightened her back, placed her glass on the floor, and ran her palms down the front of her skirt. "Explain."

From the corner of his eye, he noticed the flare-up of a lit match from outside the window, in the rain, from across Van Dam Street. It came from the second-floor semi-enclosed fire stairwell of another deserted building. The end of a cigarette glowed red and the match went out.

Frank told her his situation with Amy, finishing with a shrug of his shoulders.

She squinted and bit her bottom lip. "Well, it sounds to me like your lady friend doesn't know which way she is going. Either you or him..."

"Him?" His face snapped to face her.

Instant regret played on her face. "Oh, now I've upset you. I'm sorry," she said, raising her hand to her mouth. "I thought that you...you don't...Frank, dear, when a young lady such as your friend—you said her name was Amy—when she tells you she needs time, it usually means there is someone else in her life."

He felt like such a duped fool. It felt like there was a lance impaled in his chest, it hurt so much. His mind scrambled to find a way to discredit what the woman told him. Suspicion screamed from the back of his mind like a fading voice on a subway platform as a train trundled by.

He just couldn't make out what the voice was saying.

She leaned in closer and touched his chin as she had done earlier outside. Gently, she guided his face in her direction.

"What?" Her head was lowered slightly. Her eyes playfully scanned his own. "Did she meet you when she said she would, or did she leave you stranded? Has she ignored your feelings and refused to see you when you needed her? I'm willing to wager that you were stuck in one of those unending and terrifying situations when everything depended on seeing her. For her to open her arms and take you in, to just hold you so that you knew you weren't alone made all the difference between an empty black hole and being alive."

Frank listened to the change in her voice. Her eyes were fixed on the man in the box. "Alone and insane, you felt like some untouchable wretch that no one would want, much less hold. As if you were a ghost and she saw right through you. Your feelings were of no concern to her." Her eyes fell to some new place in the loft, but her mind and heart were outside of it. "The indifference was staggering...wasn't it?"

He watched and listened, but was unsure if she was relating what he had been through or if she was recalling something that had happened to her. His eyes followed the path of hers and found they were fixed on the man in the box. Frank awkwardly moved his hand onto hers. He gave it a soft and warm squeeze.

She snapped out of her trance.

Something rubbing against his leg snatched his attention. He looked down and saw the little black cat.

"She likes you," the woman said. "That's a good sign because she doesn't care for anyone but me."

The cat looked up, surveyed the layout of the couch, and leapt onto the spot between them. Poking its nose at Frank's hand, it rubbed the side of its head on his knuckles. Then the cat stepped back, eyed him with suspicion, and walked over to the woman.

Frank heard that clock's faint ticking.

His eyes wandered again and still could not find it. Again he noticed the woman's foot. Her left leg was crossed over her right leg. Her dangling left foot bobbed in time with the unseen clock.

Tick, up, tock, down, tick, up, tock, down….

He watched the foot bob and, from the corner of his eye, saw her twirl her hair again. The strand of long hair wrapped around her index and middle fingers as her thumb moved around them. The ticking clock, her bobbing foot, and the throbbing light in the space…all transfixed him with a growing sense of ease as he sat back comfortably on the couch. That nagging uneasiness and suspicion from earlier had disappeared.

For the first time since he could remember, he didn't feel anxious. Not nervous, or depressed, or even the slightest bit manic. Instead, he was calm and clear. There were no running, racing thoughts in his head; his mind was a blank canvas.

Something touched his knee. He looked down and saw her hand. He watched it move up his leg. The fingertips gently glided along his inner thigh. Gently, she took his glass and placed it on the floor. Then she shifted over the couch, straddling him.

His inhibitions melted completely and his mind was still. Her green eyes beamed into his as she released a soft laugh. She smiled, draping her arms around his neck. Her fingers interlocked behind his head and she tilted her head to one side like a playful puppy. She placed a small, soft kiss on his lips. She eyed him, kissed him again, smiling widely. For the first time, Frank saw in her mouth what she had so far kept from view; at the corners of her curled lips were two pointed incisors that extended longer than any of her other teeth.

A fire raged in her green eyes as she writhed gently. She took her time as she ran her fingertips down his face. Her middle finger glided down his nose. Her other hand grasped his throat. Gently, she rolled his head to one side, peppering his neck with small, soft kisses. Her hands massaged his chest as she nibbled his ear.

When he felt the pinch on his neck, he fell into a womb-like state as if drugged. He winced only for a fraction of a second, and every problem, head-ache, concern, anxiety, and fear he ever had suddenly evaporated. His eyelids fluttered. Then, like the falling of a curtain, they fell shut.

CHAPTER 11

The door to Tommy's apartment opened and Anne-Marie stepped in first. She could have closed her eyes and found her way with no problem because the layout was practically the same as all the other apartments in the neighborhood, a railroad flat in a walk-up. Tommy was lucky because his family had two connecting apartments, which meant they had the entire floor. The space was narrow and crowded.

He led her to his bedroom where she took a seat on the edge of his unmade mess of a bed. She placed her hands on her knees and let her eyes wander the bedroom. The walls were a collage of posters of long-haired guys on stages holding instruments. Some she recognized like one of the Rolling Stones, another of Black Sabbath with a young Ozzy Osbourne, The Ramones, and a black-and-white photograph of David Lee Roth with one leg stretched across the other three members of Van Halen. She didn't recognize any of the other bands. She turned around and saw over the headboard Tommy had taped a life-size cardboard-cutout bust of Donna Summer in a white dress, holding a microphone. Anne-Marie smiled because she remembered when, a few summers before, Tommy and Moe came running down Sullivan Street telling everyone how they stole it from a record store on Eighth Street. Anne-Marie knew the real story because Moe told her. The record store manager was throwing it out to make room for a new display, and Tommy just happened to be there.

The kitchen light went off and Tommy came into the bedroom. He switched on the night-table light to a low dim. He whipped his shirt from his shoulder to the floor, flipped his mane behind his ears, and lay back on the bed. He lightly ran his finger along her arm.

"That story about you and Cupid," she said.

"Yes."

"Is that the story you tell Donna Summer over there when you fantasize about getting her up here?"

He was about to argue the point, but then stopped. He figured he'd be better off not saying anything.

She took his hand and gently turned it over so that she could trace his lifeline with the tip of her finger. Her fingertip gently slithered down his hand, following the line, and then stopped. His heart pumped, his mouth was dry, and his lips quivered. He had waited years for this moment.

"I've predicted your whole life," she said.

"Oh, yeah? How's it end?"

"You'll be murdered by a jealous husband."

"That's a hell of a thing to say!" He attempted to rise up on his elbows, but Anne-Marie scrambled on top of him like a cat and pinned his shoulders to the bed with her knees. She rested the tips of her heels on the insides of his forearms and grabbed his face and squeezed his cheeks together so that his lips popped out like a chicken's beak.

"Oh, God! Thith thuckth," he moaned. "You're finally touching me, but it'th not the way I want you to. Thtill I'm jutht glad you're on top of me." He tried to move his arms, but the best he could do was make them squirm.

"Shhh!" She pointed her finger in his face. "Just be quiet for once and let someone else do the talking, big mouth. You used to be a good guy, but right now you're not much better than a piece of shit, Tommy. A real rat bastard at that."

"Where's this coming from?"

"So many places. Let's start with that Van Tassel witch Frank's been seeing. I know you made a move on her. Don't even try to deny that you made a play for her because I know you did."

"How do you know that?"

"Because I know you, Tommy."

"So?"

"So it's pretty sleazy, don't you think. Something tells me it blew up in your face, though, but let's go back even further to that night I came to your gig. Remember?"

"Yeah, sure. What of it?"

"You took me to the movies."

"I took you to a movie and that makes me a piece of shit? The only reason I took you was because you thought it was so funny that everyone said Ricardo Montalbán looked just like Moe and Gloria's Uncle Manny."

"And that's why I went, fuckhead. You think I really wanted to see a *Star Trek* movie?"

He weighed it in his head. "What do I know?" he pleaded. "Let me get this straight, you're mad at me for taking you to a *Star Trek* movie? Had I known, I would've said, 'Let's see *Rocky III*...or *E.T....*'"

"Wrong, bozo, and it's not even because you turned into an octopus five minutes after the movie started."

"You sound mad about that, too. What was I supposed to do? I thought you were into it." His face turned a beet red and the veins in his head started to bulge. "It's not like I got very far, if you remember."

"But the worst part is you're a liar. You knew Frank and I had this little thing going between us, you jealous putz. I'd flirt with him and he'd get all shy and stare at his feet so I couldn't see him blush. That's right, Tommy, I'm a flirt, not a tease. So you set up Frank with that Van Tassel tramp on the one night you knew I would be there because you were afraid, God forbid, that Frank might get more attention than you. "

"And you're mad at me?"

"Don't act so surprised, Tommy. You'd screw over your own mother to squirm your way in here." She brought her hands together by touching her thumbs and index fingers and placed them beneath her waistline. The empty space between her hands made an upside down spade. "You remember when you got involved with that skank from Alphabet City and her boyfriend and all his friends came looking for you? Who stood by you? Who took the brunt of that beating while you hid underneath a car? It was Frank, you dick."

"He broke that one guy's nose. Frank's got quite a right hook."

She pressed her weight down on him. "Where was Moe?"

He moaned. "He said something about having to watch a pinball tournament for school or something," he said.

She rattled off some more names and asked where they were the day of the beating.

"Are you done?"

She just beat her stare into his eyes a little bit longer. "Almost. Right now you should be helping him out, but what are you doing? You're trying to get between my legs."

"It's a noble cause, Anne-Marie." He looked like he might start crying at any moment. "I'm just so weak. Hold me!"

She wasn't amused. "Know what the difference between you and Frank is?"

"Tell me."

"You're gorgeous, Tommy. I'll give you that much."

"I appreciate you saying that. I really do."

"Don't," she said. "Here's the difference, schmuck: you're gorgeous, a real Barbie doll, but Frank is beautiful. That's right, Tommy, he's beautiful. He's the kind of guy a girl like me would take a bullet for and that pisses you off. He takes care of you. He always has, and you shit on him every chance you get because you're jealous of him. It's no secret, Einstein; he used to fight for you to stay in that band, but now he can't get away from you fast enough. Nobody fought for you the way he did, Tommy. Not that record producer, not your manager or even your shorter half Moe. And you know what? They're right. You know you're getting left behind and can't stand it. So rather than help your friend when he needs it, you figure if he stays down long enough he'll miss the boat and be tied to you forever. You're as bad as those girls that trick their boyfriends into getting them pregnant so the guy can't leave."

He didn't say anything. Suddenly whatever pain he felt in his forearms was replaced by a dull and edgy feeling in his chest.

"Who knows, Tommy, maybe one night when I'm bored enough, hard up, or if the planets are in the right alignment and there's a full moon, or maybe one night when I just don't care anymore I'll let you between my legs. You used to be a good guy and I'd like to think that you could be again, but right now a lay is all you're probably good for." She rolled off him and took her seat at the edge of the bed again.

He swallowed hard and covered his face with his hands. "Don't say that, Anne-Marie. I'm a good person."

She took his hand and squeezed it. "Be a stand-up guy like you used to be, and take care of your friend."

He clutched his hair, nodded, and said he would.

She pulled her hand out of his. "Now to satisfy my curiosity." She reached for the lump between his legs and gave it a thoughtful grip. She nodded as she stood up. "What do you know, it is pretty big." She leaned over and gave him a kiss on the cheek. "Good night, gorgeous. Oh, before I leave, you mind if I grab a jar of your sauce? I promised my mother I would."

"In the kitchen."

CHAPTER 12

It took about ten minutes after Anne-Marie left him high and dry before Tommy's conscience really got the best of him. He flipped his Van Halen T-shirt back over his shoulder and headed out. He stepped off the stoop of his Sullivan Street address, lit a cigarette, and winked his eye at the statue of St. Anthony that stood over the steps of the church across the street. To his right, light traffic hissed in both directions along Houston Street.

He walked down Sullivan, crossed Spring Street, and hopped a small fence in the middle of the block between two buildings. He walked through a narrow alley between the buildings then found himself in the backyard of a Sullivan Street address. He scaled the back wall and flipped himself over so he was in the backyard of Frank's Thompson Street address. He had been doing it since the fifth grade.

He hopped onto a garbage can, reached up, and grabbed the bottom rung of the fire-escape ladder. He pulled himself up and over so he was on the private little balcony outside Frank's bedroom. He tapped on the glass and waited.

A few minutes passed, but it felt like an hour, and he grew impatient. "What the fuck already!" Tommy rapped his knuckles against the window. He tried to peer in, but the lights were off.

The sound of a window being yanked open rang out. "Tommaso!" an elderly woman shouted in an Italian dialect from the second story of the adjacent building. "What's the matter with you? It's late. People are sleeping."

"Sorry, Mrs. Pastore. I'm looking for Frank, but he's not answering the door."

"Use the telephone like a normal person!" she said. "And put your clothes on!"

The window slammed back down. He made a sour face and put his shirt on. Then he climbed down and left the way he came.

He tried calling Frank's phone from the pay phone on the corner of Spring and Thompson Streets, but all it did was ring endlessly. The neighborhood was quiet and still and Tommy didn't notice another soul on the street. He slammed the phone down in a huff, scooped his dime out of the coin return, and headed down Thompson Street to Frank's building.

He stepped up to the front door and was about to press the buzzer when a hand gripped his shoulder with the strength of vise and spun him around. Before he knew it, Tommy's back was slammed up against the wall of the doorway and a cop's nightstick was pressed underneath his chin. Tommy couldn't get a good look at the cop's mocha colored face as his patrolman's cap was pulled down over his eyes.

"You Balistrieri?" the officer said.

"I know all us ginzos look alike—" Tommy flinched as the cop smacked the top of his head. He wished he thought before he spoke as he saw the name *Washington* on the cop's name plate.

"Let's see some ID. Driver's license. Now! Let's go." He had a hard face and cold eyes and was taller than Tommy by at least two inches. He had a heavy hand and at least twenty more pounds of muscle, too, but he wasn't three or four years older than Tommy.

"I don't have a driver's license," Tommy snapped and then winced as the cop smacked the top of his head again.

"We need to see some identification," another cop, a woman, said as she stepped out from behind the brute cop. She spoke in an even, nonthreatening, but authoritative tone. "Otherwise, I have to assume you're who we're looking for." She was a petite and fit woman with three white stripes on each of her sleeves. She placed her hand on the other officer's shoulder. "It's OK, officer. You can step back."

Begrudgingly the officer stepped back as he looked Tommy over.

"That's not him," a voice familiar to Tommy said.

It was Lonnie, Frank's neighbor from the fourth floor. He was a short, stocky man in his late fifties with a scruffy salt-and-pepper beard. In one hand, he held a paper coffee cup and his house keys, and a hardcover book was tucked between his rib cage and arm. He was a nocturnal sort of person, and his coloring was a testament to it. Only two months earlier, he retired after thirty years with Ma Bell. The last fifteen of those years, he worked a midnight-to-eight-a.m. shift. Tommy had known the man for as long as he could remember.

"That's Tommy Santalesa. You may want to arrest him. A few people around here would be glad if you did, but that's not Frank Balistrieri, Sergeant."

She turned back to Tommy with a thoughtful stare.

Tommy looked at her badge. Her nameplate read, *Araya*.

"Where is he?" The other cop stepped in with his palm raised to Tommy's chest.

"If I knew where he was, would I be here?" Tommy asked.

"Maybe you're picking something up for him. Maybe he asked you to get him something."

"He wouldn't be ringing the buzzer then," Sergeant Araya said as if she was thinking out loud. She stepped forward and handed Tommy a white business card. "If you see him, I strongly advise you call me right away."

Tommy and Lonnie waited for the cops to get back in their cruiser.

When the car pulled away, Tommy asked, "You know something I don't, Lonnie?"

Lonnie gave Tommy a bewildered look. "Have you been asleep all day? Hold this." He handed his coffee cup to Tommy, reached for his newspaper. He opened it to the right page and handed it to Tommy as he took his coffee back.

It was the same edition of the paper Tommy had read earlier. Tommy scanned the small article and saw the picture of Amy Van Tassel to its side. "So she's missing. Anyone who's met her knows she's a poser and a flake. She's an actress, Lonnie."

"There were two other cops waiting right here out in front since about four o'clock this afternoon. They had the super open up Frank's apartment earlier and they went inside. They didn't find him."

"I don't follow you."

"Come on, Tommy, you're smarter than that." Lonnie looked away for a moment, not sure if Tommy was telling the truth or just playing dumb. "He's dating that Van Tassel girl who also just so happens to be missing."

"So what're you saying?"

Lonnie looked up for a moment, rubbed his chin, and let out a small, knowing chuckle. "I'm sure you can figure this out."

Tommy stared at him blankly. Finally, a thought clicked in. "What, you think they ran off together?"

"I'm just saying…"

"No way. You're nuts. That makes no sense. He's two steps from being a rock star. He's on the verge of…Everything's going his way, Lonnie." Tommy thought it over again. "He's not going to piss it all away for some girl. Even that one."

Lonnie shrugged his shoulders in defeat. "What can I say?" He unlocked and then pushed open the front door. "He's not here, but I'll bet you my pension it won't just be the cops coming around tomorrow."

"Huh?"

"Maybe FBI and probably a wad of private investigators, reporters, and a ton of TV cameras. So, if you have any idea, even the smallest inclination of where he may be, I suggest you find him, Tommy."

Tommy racked his brains. "He's a homebody, Lonnie. He doesn't go anywhere."

"He went somewhere, kid, because he's not here."

Chapter 13

Tommy walked to the corner and then jaywalked across Broome Street to an all-night deli on the corner of Sullivan Street. As he leaned down and stuck his arm into the refrigerator for a pint of orange juice, he noticed a shadow stretch across the floor and lay itself over his arm and the refrigerator. He appeared like he always did at night. He showed up twitching and blinking like he was suffering a long state of anxiety, a haggard and burnt-out-looking man in clothes that were too big for his malnourished frame. He wore a dingy white T-shirt with a faded graphic of Mighty Mouse. His hair was long, gray, and stringy like weeds. His teeth weren't in the best shape, either, and his eyes were permanently bloodshot from sleepless nights.

He was what the cops called a skell.

Squid wasn't from the neighborhood or even a native New Yorker. He came from somewhere in New England about fifteen years before with nothing but a guitar, a lot of talent, skill, and a wicked taste for the sweet stuff that had him shackled and chained since 1969.

Tommy saw him and said, "Squid, what's shaking besides you?" Sensing the man didn't get the joke, Tommy flipped him a can of soda from the refrigerator. "It's on me."

"I know a secret," he hissed, catching the soda.

"What's that?"

Squid fumbled with the can, found the lid, and cracked it open. "Your friend..." He crinkled his face as the carbonation burned his nose. "She's been watching him…watching him for a long time. She didn't know…she didn't see me." He raised his hand like a claw and made a gripping gesture. "Tonight she got him."

Tommy became jealous because he figured Squid was high and there was nothing else Tommy wanted to be more at that moment. Tommy sidestepped him and walked to the counter where he slapped down a few dollars. "Somebody got Moe?" he asked as he scooped up his change.

Squid shook his head as his eyes darted in all directions while his teeth ground. "Not Moe. Frank I'm talking about."

"Frank?" Tommy asked and took notice of Squid's shifting and twitching. *He seems nervous*, Tommy thought. "What're you talking about?"

Squid looked away and then turned back quickly. "Can I have a dollar? I need a dollar. Can I have a dollar…please?" He stuck out his unwashed hand.

Tommy rolled his eyes, dug into his front pocket, and dropped a crumpled dollar bill into Squid's palm.

With one hand, Squid folded the bill over and rubbed the two ends together. "I know because I watched her. She doesn't know I was there."

"Who?"

"The witch."

Tommy pulled off his T-shirt and used it to pat down the back of his neck. He was careful not to snag the delicate gold chain that a matching crucifix hung from. "I have no idea what you're talking about, Squid, but I'm glad Frank's finally giving up on that Van Tassel chick and moving on." Tommy stuffed his hard pack of Navajo Lights cigarettes between his flat stomach and the top of his jeans. He whipped his shirt onto his right shoulder. "It's too hot for this. I'm going home to take a shower."

On any other night it would have ended there, but Squid wouldn't let it go. He insisted on following Tommy and trailed behind him like some spastic and confused lapdog. Tommy had to play connect-the-dots to follow what he was saying.

"She's not a witch," he said. "She's like a witch. What I mean is she comes out of a shadow…no, that's not right…she is the shadow of a bigger shadow… where she hides."

Tommy was self-conscious as they crossed Spring Street. He didn't want anyone he knew to get the idea that he was hanging out with Squid. After taking a look to be sure that no one he knew was around, Tommy nodded to let Squid know he was paying attention. They crossed over to the west side of Sixth Avenue, stopped in a small poorly lit park, and each took a seat across from each other at a weather-worn concrete chess table beneath the trees.

Tommy plopped the pack of Navajo Lights onto the chess table. He pulled out of two cigarettes and gave one to Squid. "How do you know this?"

Taking the cigarette from Tommy's hand, Squid said, "I saw her...one night...just about every night. She comes out a shadow, and the shadow comes out of that old building on Van Dam Street." He lit the cigarette with a shaking hand. "But there's more..."

The streetlamp above cast a dim, but warm and whitish glow on them. Dark shadows, only half impressions as if a mask of darkness had shrouded the features it wanted to remain hidden. Slowly and steadily a chill crept up Tommy's spine that made the hairs on his neck and arms stand straight up. He heard a stirring in the trees around them and the rustling of limbs and their leaves. Then, through the streetlamp's whitish glow, a shadow, for a moment, passed.

Squid stopped his twitching and looked at Tommy with soft, wide eyes. Then they became two slits. "She's trying to nurture him...to cultivate him, but he won't be alive anymore."

"How do you know this?" Tommy was getting angry. "Where did you see this?"

"Through the window of that old factory or whatever it was. You know, that place that's been abandoned since forever...that place the old people used to talk about."

There was another rustling in the trees. This time it was louder and it caught Squid's attention. He looked up and his face turned to one of fear. He jumped up, like a frightened child, and walked away at a rapid pace with his head bowed down. "I shouldn't be telling you this...it's not right...she's been good to me..."

Tommy called after him, but he kept moving. Tommy sprang up, ran after him, and grabbed him by the arm. "What do you mean he won't be alive anymore? Is she trying to kill him?"

Squid, still looking down, shook his head. "Worse than kill him."

Tommy repeated the question and tightened his grip on Squid's arm.

Squid's face shot straight up to look Tommy dead in the eye. "He'll be un-dead." He pulled away from Tommy and ran away.

Tommy stood, stunned, on the corner for a few moments as he watched Squid's body become smaller and smaller until it disappeared above Houston Street. He mulled over what Squid had told him, but the whole story was too weird.

CHAPTER 14

Frank shot up straight with a gasp. His body glistened with sweat, and cold chills danced along his arms and spine. He didn't feel right. He felt sick and his stomach was a tight knot, but he was hungry. He wanted to eat, but that could wait. He had to meet Amy and he sensed that he was already late, but he had to get moving. He reached for the light over his night table and fell out of the bed. He lay on his back on the hardwood floor with a spinning head in the darkness.

He had the strangest revelation.

This isn't my apartment, he thought. *Oh, God, where am I?* The thought trailed off in his mind, echoing as it faded. It was then that he remembered. He remembered the woman, going home with her, but the rest were only flashes of images, snapshots, and fleeting sound bites.

His head pounded and his neck hurt, but he managed to sit up.

Frank rubbed the back of his neck and then stopped. He felt something along his neck. It stung to the touch. Two dots, like inverted mosquito bites.

He heard noises from the dark and whispering voices. He caught glimpses of moving shapes that shifted in the dark and heard the sound of shuffling feet. Unable to stand, Frank crawled along the floor with the light of a few remaining candles that flickered to guide him.

Panic-stricken, Frank—despite the spinning head and stomach knots — stood up, leaned on the bed for support, and found his pants. He put them on, frantically searched by touch for his sneakers, and found them. He didn't bother looking for his socks and abandoned any thought of looking for his shirt. Like a sick blind man, Frank stumbled in the dark with his arms outstretched like feelers. In the distance, he made out the impression of the doorframe by the flickering of the remaining candlelight.

A hand grasped his forearm. He tried to pull back, but the grip was too tight. In that remaining wobbling light, Frank caught sight of three men stumbling with widely spread arms and moving in a jerky fashion. With their own arms also extended as feelers, they reached for anything. They surrounded him with sorrowful and lost-sounding moans as they reached and grabbed.

He jumped back in fear, seeing that the moaning men's eyes were gouged. His back hit the wall with a thud. Hearing this, they reached for him. Frank reeled back again, hit the wall, and stumbled as it gave. The hot and sticky air wrapped around him like blanket. It was a back door he accidentally swung open so unexpectedly that he fell backward onto the wrought-iron landing of the outside fire escape. He tried to regain his balance but failed. He spun, tripped, and fell down the flight of rusted and corroded steps.

CHAPTER 15

Tommy stuck his index finger and thumb into his mouth and blew out an air-raid siren of a whistle so loud that it was probably heard across the Atlantic. "Squid!" he shouted. "It's me, Tommy!" He stood before the building that Squid said he slept in. At the end of the block, to his left, Hudson Street looked empty and dead. To his right was Varick Street. The only sign of life was the occasional cab or delivery truck that headed toward the tunnel or further down to Canal Street.

He looked behind him and saw, across the street, the building Squid told him Frank was in. He eyed the dirty, high, and rectangular windows that lined the place. There was no door or anything to indicate an entrance, just an ugly but sinister-looking excuse for a tree that loomed to the side of an arched driveway with its bare and contorted branches outstretched.

The driveway caught his eye, and as he turned to walk across the street, he flipped a cigarette to the curb.

Tommy stood before a gaping black hole that was high and wide enough for a truck to drive through. It was the driveway of the old foundry at 50 Van Dam. Tommy knew that the driveway led to a courtyard behind the building. He also knew that was where all the area junkies, drunks, and assorted loons spent their nights in the summer whenever the cops chased them out of Washington Square Park. Like his private handball court a few blocks away, it was perfect, out of the way and in a part of the neighborhood that normal people stayed away from after hours. He knew he would find Squid there if he could only bring himself to step into that pitch-black tunnel. He looked back at that tree, at its bare, outstretched, contorted limbs, and couldn't shake the feeling that it stared at him hatefully. With a shiver, he looked forward again and stared into the wall of black before him. *I should've just hopped the fence on the other side, around the back,* he thought. His left hand touched the small gold crucifix that hung around his neck, and with a pounding heart he stepped inside.

Chapter 16

Frank tumbled down to the loading dock and then rolled off the side. His back smacked the wet blacktop. Pebbles, grit, tiny shards of glass, and a bottle cap pinched and pierced his skin. He lay there for a moment to catch his breath. He inhaled deeply and rose to his feet. With a spinning head, he leaned on the loading dock for support.

He looked at his surroundings in the courtyard and tried to remember. He remembered waiting for Amy, standing in the rain, and then meeting that woman…whoever she was. It started to come back to him. He remembered bumping into her, walking her home, and then the woman inviting him upstairs.

The moans of the blind men stole his attention. He looked up to the fire escape and the open door he had come through. The throbbing oranges and yellows were dimming from within. On the landing, outside the door, two of the men had fallen on their faces and struggled to raise themselves. Then the silhouetted image of the third man filled the doorway.

The image of the woman handing him the glass came to him. He remembered sitting on the couch, the strand of hair her fingers slithered around, and the foot bobbing gently, so soothing as it rose and fell as if riding a wave. He remembered the ticking clock that he couldn't find, her hand as it touched his knee, and that jingling sound her bracelets made.

Those moans from above turned to screams of panic. The silhouette of the man in the doorway struggled to get out of the doorway, but couldn't. Like a cat trying to stay out of a box, the man's hands desperately clung to both sides of the doorframe.

The two men on the landing had risen to their feet, but lost their balance and tumbled down the flight of wrought-iron steps. They hit the landing below in a clump and then blindly scurried off the loading dock, not knowing or caring what may be in front of them. A bloodcurdling shriek came from the top of the steps as the man was lifted off his feet and then sailed through the air.

The body flew over Frank's head and hit the ground with a crunching thud. Frank saw the other two men squirm on the ground beneath the weight of the thrown victim. He looked away and above to the doorway where he saw the woman's silhouette occupy the entrance and then vanish. Something black moved and then seemed to drip down the steps to the loading dock like a hive or an oil slick on the surface of the water. It moved smoothly down the brick of the loading dock and got lost in the darkness and camouflaged within the blacktop.

CHAPTER 17

As if poured in reverse, the woman's form rose up from the blacktop with the three men writhing at her feet. The jingling of her metal bracelets rang out as she reached down to clutch one by the throat, and she lifted him off the ground with all the effort of hoisting a rag doll from a toy box. The man's feet kicked like a panic-stricken chicken held upside down by its ankles. Then, with the speed of a shark, she pulled the body to her and attacked its throat. His head rolled back, and Frank saw the man's empty eye sockets were two blackened pits. The body collapsed like a deflated balloon and became a drained chalk white. The blood, as it ran down her cheeks and neck, looked black as oil in the poor light. She tossed the deflated and chalk-white corpse as if it were an empty lobster shell. It hit the blacktop and shattered into a cloud of gray ash.

It was pathetic and heartbreaking to watch. He wanted to run but was paralyzed by the fear of being seen by her. He crouched down to a near squat and pressed himself against the loading wall, hoping to remain unnoticed.

She wiped her lower lip with the tip of her middle finger and reached down for another body. The man was spun around so that she was behind him as she draped her arm across his chest and then attacked his throat. The body jerked and the mouth made a gurgling noise. When she was finished she let the body fall. Frank watched the man's chalk-white head smack the ground and crumble like a piecrust.

The third man, on his back, blindly kicked at her. A smile—so devious and wicked that it reminded Frank of a rat's—stretched across her face as she crouched over the kicking man. Her teeth were two rows of interlocked daggers that gleamed, and he could see that her fingertips had become longer and sharper, like daggers themselves. As she grabbed a wad of the man's hair at the back of his head, her eye caught Frank huddled by the wall. Her body collapsed and sank into the blacktop.

Frank saw the blacktop ripple as the hive moved toward him. It was before him in an instant and sprouted into the form of that woman.

"Love," she said as she knelt and took his hand. "It's too soon for you to be out..."

He wanted to move away but didn't have the courage. He saw, in the background, her third victim rise to his feet, stumble, and shuffle away like a baby taking its first steps.

CHAPTER 18

Inside the dark and dank tunnel, Tommy's skin was like a canvas written in braille it had so many goose bumps. The hairs on the back of his neck stood as erect as insect antennae. The tunnel felt a mile long. He held his flip-top cigarette lighter at his side. The top was closed. He wanted to light it, but was afraid of what he might see within the arched driveway.

He thought he heard a scream and that was enough for him to stop dead in his tracks. His body tensed, and he wanted to kill Anne-Marie for her guilt trip, smack Squid for his creepy story, and slap Lonnie for his dumb insights. All he wanted to do was get out of the tunnel. He put his head down, hoped for the best, and kept walking in a straight line.

Tommy came out of the tunnel and was in the courtyard. At the far end of the courtyard, beyond the clumpy shapes of construction equipment and vehicles, he could make out the impression of a warped chain-link fence. A streetlamp off in the distance helped him a little to see the redbrick building, a place he had walked a million times and never bothered to look at. He saw the loading dock stretch the building's entire length. Then his eyes stopped as they came across the open door and the blackness within. A heavy dread weighed down on him.

His hands shook as he fidgeted to light a cigarette, and he'd barely inhaled the first drag when he saw a shape in the dark shuffle his way. It moved in a zigzag and seemed to almost fall over with each step, but somehow managed to continue. Tommy could already tell it wasn't Squid.

"Hey, man," Tommy said, flagging the guy over. "I'm looking for Squid. Is he around?"

The shuffling shape was close enough for Tommy to see the man's face in the dim light. He jumped back and his jaw dropped as he noticed the thin red slash that ran the width of the man's face and cut across his eyes. The man's wild and crazed hands reached out for Tommy.

"Help!" the blind man cried.

A black and shapeless mass sprang up from the ground between them. Tommy jumped back, and the black mass became a woman that looked at him with a hateful stare. She hissed at him as the flickering of the tiny gold around his neck caught her eye. She turned, wrapped herself around the blind man, and vanished.

Tommy stood, dumbstruck as his heart tried to jump out of his chest. Tommy could swear the man was Charlie DeMarco. Then a pain-wrenched shriek rang out. His eyes followed the scream and he saw the woman knelt over the writhing body. When the body stopped moving, she vanished again.

Tommy froze, thinking it would come out of the darkness for him, but then he jumped at the sounds of a dog barking from behind him. Before he could turn around, a big dog blew past him with its leash trailing on the ground behind it.

"Veronica, no!" a voice shouted.

Tommy was thrown off his feet as Al Lucchese, hauling like a freight train, checked him as he ran after the dog. Lucchese didn't even look back.

CHAPTER 19

Frank was still huddled against the wall when he saw her reappear and approach him. His throat was so dry. It felt rough and sore. He smelled the blood on her skin and wanted it. His body craved it. His tongue was dry. He tried to stand on his own, but she stopped him as she knelt down beside him and brushed her hair away from her neck, taking his head gently into her hands. As she guided his head to her own neck, the vicious growls of the angry dog rang out. Her concentration was broken as she saw the big dog, a Rottweiler, charging from out of the darkness.

The dog was momentarily stunned and came to a halt as the woman evaporated. It cocked its head to one side and then turned its attention to Frank. Some instinct took over as he stood up and flung himself up on the loading dock. Clearing his head, he lay on his back trying to catch his breath. The dog rose on her hind legs and propped her paws on the loading dock. Then it turned and focused on a blackened corner along the warped chain-link fence. It turned and charged.

He saw his opportunity and took it. Frank mustered all the strength he could and threw himself onto his feet. Using the platform for balance, he moved forward with a jogging pace. From behind him, he could hear the vicious growls and shouts of the dog as it fought in that darkened corner. He picked up his pace to a stumbling run and kept moving.

And then there was silence. The dog wasn't barking anymore. He stopped, but wouldn't look back. He heard an animal's whimper, swallowed hard, and moved on with his head down.

He slammed into someone and teetered.

"Frank!" Tommy said as he tried to hold him up. "Squid said…" He saw something big come hurling through the air in their direction.

Tommy stopped talking and pulled Frank to the ground with him. Just above their head, a large, dark-colored lump soared past them, hit the blacktop with a thud, and then skidded into a wall. Tommy watched the lump wriggle, stand on all fours, and then come charging.

Tommy yanked Frank to his feet, leaned him up against the wall, and stepped in front of him. The dog approached, baring its fangs. Tommy kicked but never actually connected.

"Who's there?" a voice shouted. A bright circle of light grew bigger and more blinding as it came closer. "Jesus Christ! I should've known it was you, Tinker Bell."

The dog growled and pivoted as she tried to sidestep Tommy to get at Frank.

"Hey, Rubber, you feel like telling your date to lay off?"

Al Lucchese's knees creaked as he leaned down with a moan and picked up the leather leash. He shined the flashlight onto Frank while he adjusted the strap of the canvas bag that hung from his shoulder. "Say, what's with your friend anyway? He ain't looking too good."

"He's not feeling well." Tommy held his palm over his eye to block out the light. "He's got a summer flu."

"Summer flu, my ass!" Lucchese held the flashlight in a cocked arm to the side of his face and moved the light back and forth between them. "The two of you came down here to score some dope. That's it; I'm taking you in."

"Keep dreaming, Rubber. You're not even a cop anymore. The only place we're going is a hospital. Look at his neck. Your stupid dog bit him and now he has rabies, I bet."

"My Ronnie's clean!" He became indignant, inflamed. "I just had Doc Myers check her out the other day."

Doc Myers, Tommy thought, *that's it!* At least Tommy could buy some time before seeing the cops.

Chapter 20

"Idiot," Myers said to his reflection in the bathroom mirror. He stared at the black eye on the left side of his face and sighed. The knot in his tie was loose and pulled to one side, his collar button was undone, and the cuffs of his sleeves were rolled up his forearms. He splashed cold tap water on his face and toweled off.

He was about to step into the kitchen to get some ice or a steak for his eye when a heavy pounding came at the front door. He hesitated, rolled his eyes, and went to the pounding. He knew it was Lucchese.

He flung open the door. "You're making this a habit." Immediately he was pushed aside as Veronica pounced. Her paws hit his chest and jaw was slack as her stump of a tail wagged. Myers rubbed her neck as he eyed the scene in the doorway.

"Doc Myers, thank God you're here." Tommy pushed ahead of Lucchese, taking Frank with him. "Rubber's wife bit my friend."

Myers looked to Lucchese. "Who is this? Do I know him?"

Lucchese pulled a frown and stepped inside. "Doc, meet Tinker Bell, the neighborhood wiseass." He eyed Myers with a confused expression. "Whoa! You mix it up with someone?"

"Don't ask," Myers said as he eased Veronica back on all fours. He looked at Tommy. "Do we know each other?"

"You're Doc Myers. Everyone around here knows you."

Then it clicked for Myers. Tommy was one of those neighborhood kids that hung around the back lot smoking reefer all summer. He looked at Frank and his face turned grim. "What's with your friend?"

"Like I said, *his* dog bit him. I think he has rabies now."

"Rabies?" Myers's face fell flat and he stared at Tommy blankly. "I can assure you Veronica does not have rabies."

"See?" Lucchese stuck out his chest.

"Just the same," Tommy said as Frank's body slumped. "I'd like you to take a look at him."

Myers sighed and then leaned down to raise one of Frank's heavy eyelids. "Well, whatever it was, he took too much of it." He stood with a shrug of his shoulders. "He needs a doctor; I'm a vet. Take him to St. Vincent's."

"He didn't take anything. I told you, Rubber's dog bit him." Tommy turned Frank's head and showed Myers the points in his neck.

"That's no dog bite," Myers said as he leaned in closer. "Bring him into my office."

Once the three of them brought Frank into Myers's office, they laid him on the cot. He was nearly asleep.

Lucchese paced, rubbed the back of his neck, and breathed irritably. "It's hot in here," he moaned. "Why's the air conditioner not on?"

"It's still broken from the last time you fixed it," Myers said as he eyed over Frank. "There's a fan on the reception desk."

"Fans don't do nothing but blow the hot air all around."

Myers used his thumbs to open and close Frank eyes. He lightly slapped Frank's cheek. "Stay with me. What did you take?"

Frank only moaned.

Myers checked Frank's wrists for a pulse, then his neck, and back to the wrists. He looked at Tommy with a frustrated stare. "What did he take?"

"Nothing!" Tommy huffed.

Lucchese still paced, still huffed, and still grunted. "That's what they do, these kids. They hang out in there and try to score drugs. You should see the skells that place attracts."

"Nobody was scoring anything, Rubber," Tommy snapped as he leaned against the windowsill. He popped a cigarette into his mouth and reached for his lighter in his back pocket.

Myers heard the clink of a flip-top lighter springing open. His head snapped to Tommy. "Not in here!" he shouted. "Smoke outside." Lucchese's hovering, pacing, and huffing hit Myers's last nerve. "You, too, out!"

Chapter 21

For ten minutes, Tommy stood outside on the stoop in the hot summer air beneath those bloated and bulbous clouds. Nervously he smoked another cigarette as a wave of nerve-racking thoughts overcame him. He thought about what he saw in the courtyard, what Squid had told him, and that cop who gave him her card. What Lonnie had said repeated itself over and over like a song he couldn't get out of his head. If what Lonnie said was true about Frank and Amy running off together, then where was Amy?

He heard the door to Myers's office open with a creak and he spun around. Seeing Myers, Tommy flicked his cigarette off into the street and opened the screen door.

Myers stood in the hallway. His eyes shifted from Lucchese to Tommy and back again. He looked disappointed.

"Is my friend OK?" Tommy blurted out.

"Is this some kind of hoax the two of you are playing on me?" Myers asked as his eyes touched each of theirs. "I'm not in the mood for games."

"A hoax? Don't be stupid, Doc," Lucchese said. "Give it up already. You looked him over, checked his pulse…"

"That's right, Al. I did check his pulse. Four times to be exact."

"OK, and?"

"He doesn't have one."

"Awwwwww!" Tommy's back hit the wall, his face fell to his hands, and he slumped down to the floor.

PART TWO
A SPIRIT ON PAROLE

Chapter 1

"Squid?" Myers was beside himself. "What kind of name is Squid?"

"It's not his real name. His name's Cal."

"How do you get Squid out of Cal?"

"Well…Cal leads to calamari and then to Squid. Plus there's something very *squid* about him. If you met him you'd understand."

Myers scratched his head and rubbed his neck. He had been listening to Tommy for the past five minutes, and when he couldn't bear to hear any more of it, he blurted out, "It's a great story, kid. The devil lives in an abandoned warehouse…"

"Not the devil!" Tommy shouted. "It's a witch or…something."

Tommy sat in a slump on a ratty-looking waiting-room couch that would have fit better in a frat house. His forearms rested on his knees, and his hands fell down limply. He looked tired, felt tired, and was, in fact, overtired. He wanted to lie down, close his eyes, and forget about everything, even if for only a few minutes. The problem was that his mind and body were out of sync so that, at any moment, he would jump off the couch in a restless huff.

Myers held a sympathetic expression but remained unconvinced.

"But what I told you…and…" Tommy was dumbstruck. "Ask Rubber if you don't believe me."

"You also said you think you saw Charlie DeMarco with his eyes gouged out and then eaten by a shadow." Myers was hot and annoyed, and Tommy's story was just filling the place up with more hot air. "You see this?" Myers pointed to his left and blackened eye. "Do I look like I'm in the mood to be taken for a ride? I looked over your friend and there's nothing I can really do for him. He needs a doctor."

"He needs a priest is what I'm saying," Tommy said. "You said so yourself that he doesn't have a pulse."

Myers shook his head in a tizzy. "That doesn't mean anything. His heart rate may have slowed…"

"His heart rate may have slowed? He's not a swami."

Myers rolled his eyes, shrugged, and threw up his hands. He left Tommy in the hallway and entered his office. He flicked the light switch and checked Frank's arms for marks by running his fingers along the inside of the forearms. Then he patted down Frank's front pockets, dug into them, and found a few crumpled dollar bills.

He swung open the office door and motioned for Tommy to enter the room.

"Well?" Tommy asked.

Myers closed the door, leaned against it, and eyed Tommy skeptically. "Are you telling me the truth?"

"About what?"

"Did he take something?"

"What, like drugs? No."

"You think I don't know who you are? You and your friends have been smoking reefer in the back lot just about every morning this summer." Myers had already checked Frank, but he still had to see if there was something Tommy wasn't telling him. "If I search him…"

"You won't find anything."

"And if I search you?"

Tommy dug into his pants, pulled out the dime bag, and handed it over. "It's just weed."

Myers opened the bag and stuck his nose in it. "You know your stuff."

"You can have some if you want."

Myers smiled and handed it back. "Put it away before Lucchese sees it. For what it's worth, I believe you, but I don't know what's wrong with your friend. I don't know what bit him either. The best place for him is a hospital, so I suggest we take him to St. Vincent's in a little while." Myers leaned on his desk, crossed his ankles, and put his hands in his pockets. "Now, we've established that I know you, but how do you know me?"

Tommy made a muffled laugh. "Like, around here, who doesn't? You're Doc Myers and everyone in this neighborhood knows who you are. What, you think all those old ladies that feed you aren't going to talk about you? Damn, Doc, you've been the focus of many of their late night conversations over in Thompson Park."

"I have?" Myers wasn't sure how he felt about it.

"Uh-huh." Tommy added, "That girl you have working here...you know, the brick house..." Tommy flashed him a devilish and equally corny smile. "How are you two, you know, hitting it off?"

Myers was beside himself and uncomfortable. He stuttered, stammered, and then finally stopped thinking. "Where did you get that idea?"

"Is this a trick question? Like, she didn't give you that?" Tommy pointed to Myers's eye. "I bet she's been trying to blackmail you into taking her out, too."

Myers was suddenly stiffer and more rigid. He looked at Tommy questioningly.

"She's a neighborhood girl, Doc. I told you how the old people around here talk. Everybody in this neighborhood knows everybody. It's like a small village even though it's in the big city."

Myers scratched his head. He wanted to know more but at the same time didn't.

"First thing you have to learn, Doc, is that a lot of these old birds don't really have a lot to do. Outside of church activities and housework, they like to sit around and gossip, but not in a bad way. They don't mean anything by it. It's just a way to pass the time. Like I said, you've been the topic of many of their conversations in the park at night after dinner. Like, last summer when you first showed up and nobody knew what to make of you. They thought you might be gay or asexual, but a few months later Richie Lantieri told some people he saw you and that ass monkey Lucchese leaving Wong's House of Pleasure all red faced and giggly."

Myers's face became so flushed it nearly burned. *They knew about that?* He figured it best to play dumb. "Wong's House of what?"

"You know, the Chinese whorehouse…oops, I mean, massage parlor down on Canal Street." Tommy picked up on Myers's embarrassment. "Don't sweat it, Doc. At least now they know that you're alive. Besides, according to half these kooks it's better you paid to be with a woman than to be with a man for free. Not that they'd condemn you for it or anything, but…"

"But what?"

"They'd feel sorry for you."

"Why?"

"Well, outside of not getting into heaven because you're not Catholic, they'd think you're really going to hell for being with a man. When word got out that Moe and Gloria's cousin Victor had a thing for guys, those old ladies lit so many candles it was like a bonfire in St. Anthony's." Tommy pulled a cigarette out of his pack. "They said so many prayers they gave God a headache."

"Not in here," Myers said, pointing to the cigarette.

"I know, I know."

"Before you go outside, I have a question."

"Shoot."

"Why do you call him Rubber?"

Tommy looked at Myers like he was crazy, as if the answer was so simple. "Because he's a scumbag."

CHAPTER 2

Veronica was chin down on the kitchen floor with a bored look on her face at Lucchese's feet. Her ears perked at the whine of the opening and then closing of the front screen door, so she walked to the room's entrance to have a look. She saw Myers and leisurely walked toward him. Further, in the distance and outside the front door, she saw Tommy smoking on the front porch.

The pitter-patter of her nails tapping on the hardwood floor caught Myers's attention. He was heading upstairs to the kennel when he heard Veronica's steps. He turned and saw her staring back with a tilted head. He patted his thigh and she trotted down the stretch of floor wedged between Myers's office and the stairs. Reaching him, she pounced.

He rubbed her shoulders and gently lowered her down on all fours. He knelt and unclipped her leather harness, and as he did this, he felt something fall into his palm. He stood up and stared at what looked like a snapped fingernail about three inches long with a pointed tip and a sharp center edge. He tried to bend it, but it was firm.

Veronica playfully pounced again and broke his concentration.

She sat back down on her hindquarters as her tongue dangled and her tail wagged. Myers knelt down again and looked her over with searching eyes as his hands gently patted her head. He looked into her wide eyes and slid his palm along her tight muscular body. His overview determined she was fine, but she had tangled with something. Judging by the nail in his hand, he knew she was lucky, but he couldn't tell what she had mixed it up with. He stood up and stuffed the nail into his front pocket.

"Come on, girl, it's sleepy time." He patted his hip as he led her up the stairs.

CHAPTER 3

From deep within the darkness it called to her.

Her eyes shot open and her ears perked like an alert Doberman. It was a familiar voice that she heard often, but just ignored. Yet now she struggled to ignore it. Like a distant and fading ghost, it did more than call; it beckoned.

She scowled and tried to put it out of her head.

It was there when she came home, but it was quiet then. Well behaved even, but now that chocolate cookie on a plate in the kitchen wouldn't stop its moaning.

Flat on her back with her hands crossed over her stomach, Cynthia had mulled over, for the past hour, her date with Doc Myers. Her index finger tapped out a beat and her forehead was creased into a frown. Her lips formed a sour and tense pout.

One of her cats—she didn't know which, Spot or Jerome—was asleep by the side of her head.

She couldn't sleep. It was too hot, her date tanked, and that cookie wouldn't shut up. So what stopped her from her getting up and eating the cookie? It was the two years she had spent keeping off all the fat that had left her alone and dateless every Saturday night all throughout high school and three years after graduation. Her friends, all of them, went out on dates and did all the things only the fat girls missed out on. Cynthia hated what she had been, hated what she had looked like, and hated most being the fat girl because it meant being left with no options. It meant she could only take what had been given to her, whether she liked it or not.

"Stupid cookie," she muttered as she analyzed her date. God, what an embarrassment it was. It was if someone had placed the most beautiful birthday cake before her and it blew up in her face as she tried to blow out the candles.

She tried to figure out what she had done wrong. Had she missed something, some subtle sign that Myers had sent her way? He met her outside her building and they strolled along together until they reached Mulberry Street in Little Italy. They ate at a nice, crowded, and tight-fitting place. They shared a bottle of red wine that she ended up drinking most of. She made sure not to eat everything on her plate, but made up for it in water.

Although, Myers did seem uptight, the way he shook his leg, tapped his fingers on the table, and looked for the waiter from the minute they sat down to the second the check arrived. Nervously his eyes had scanned the menu, and then when he folded over its cover he shot a glance at the waiter and then to her. He shook his head then gave a slight nod and said, "Whatever you're having."

That wasn't even the worst of it either. The worst part was that he looked so good. No, he looked beautiful dressed in that blue suit that highlighted his icy blue eyes. Underneath he wore a crisp white shirt and a blue tie. His hair was nicely combed and he wore a nice gold watch instead of that beat-up old Timex he wore in the office.

The dinner conversation had a lopsided rhythm to it, too. It varied from lulls of silence where Myers looked around the restaurant like a self-conscious teenager out on a date with the fat girl to him making boring small talk as he nodded stupidly and forced out fake smiles.

Cynthia didn't realize how much wine she'd had until they were outside after dinner. She was a little tipsy as they walked along Broome Street. Subtly she reached for his hand as they walked, but missed it as he raised his arm to fix his glasses. When she curled up next to him to take his arm, he was stiff as a board and didn't even bother to look at her. Finally, when they reached the corner at West Broadway, she stepped in front of him and turned to face him with a bright smile.

"What would you say if I asked you to kiss me?" She practically closed her eyes and puckered up.

He made a face. "You've had too much to drink."

Cynthia's mouth curled itself into a hybrid of a smirk and pout. Her hands crossed over each other just above her knees as she rose to the balls of her feet so that in her heels she was just a little bit taller than Myers.

"I like you, Myers," she said as her eyelids fell halfway and met him with a smoldering stare. "I really do."

Myers did not melt or so much as flinch. "You like an idea, Cynthia."

It was the *way* he said it that hurt so much. As if she were just some stupid child.

She remembered feeling her face contort into a nasty snarl that was matched only by the rage that boiled within. Her eyes became two narrow slits, her jaw tightened, and suddenly her leg twitched. Slave to the impulse twitch, Cynthia kicked him dead center in his shin.

"Ow!" he yelled as he hopped on one foot while he held his shin. He looked at her like a scared and confused puppy.

Her eyes never widened. She swung her bag at the upper part of his arm near the shoulder.

"Easy," he said while he still hopped on one foot. "I bruise like a peach."

The rage boiled more still and she felt that anger seep through the corners of her slitted eyes.

He backed away with a hop. "What did I do?"

Maybe he's dumb, maybe he's borderline retarded, or maybe he's just a dick, she remembered thinking. At that moment, though, she didn't care any longer. All Cynthia knew was that her words, her affections, and her advances had been met with nothing more than rejection. Her right hand curled into a tight and hard fist. She hauled off and wailed him in his left eye.

Myers stopped bobbing, teetered for a moment, and then fell over on the sidewalk.

"That may not have been the best way to handle it," she muttered in the darkness of her bedroom. "Still..." She shook her head, thinking about how she had dolled herself up for the date in a new deep-red dress with spaghetti straps. Her heels really made the made the most of her well-defined calves. She had pulled her hair up and kept it perfectly in place with a bow-shaped clip.

Damn! She looked so hot, and for once she knew it, too.

The dress was now flung over the chair near her bed. It hung there lifeless, limp, and drained of any life it had earlier in the evening. Just thinking about it made her angry and sad. The shoes were scattered on the floor, and the right shoe—the one she used to kick Myers with—was broken. The heel had snapped as she stormed off. She'd almost twisted her ankle on it as she walked, but lost her balance and the heel gave out as part of the deal.

"What a bust," she hissed out as she got out of bed.

Cynthia wanted a glass of water, so she tiptoed into the kitchen and pulled down on the little chain to turn on the kitchen light.

"*Surprise!*" the chorus rang out.

The whole gang was there. Her old friends French pastry, cupcakes, and that chocolate chip cookie all danced and cheered on the table. From inside the fridge and freezer came the muffled cheers of more friends as they danced and partied like it was a Friday at Danceteria up on Thirtieth Street. The guest list included butter, frozen French fries, ice cream, and whole milk just to name a few.

Her hand reached forward and her fingertip grazed the cookie. She picked it up and it seemed to giggle it was so happy.

"Fuck off," she said as she whipped it, like a Frisbee, out the open kitchen window and into the back lot of her building. Then she flipped her middle finger to the French pastry and the cupcakes and got herself a glass of water.

She walked the narrow length of the flat, took a seat on the windowsill, and looked out her window through the bars of the fire escape to the street below. There was a small transistor radio on the windowsill with a strand of telephone cross-connection wire that was wrapped around the stub of metal where the antennae had snapped off. The other end of the wire was connected to the water pipe that ran vertically through all six floors of the building. She turned it on but kept the volume low.

"*...you give us twenty-two minutes and we'll give you the world. At the sound of the tone, Ten-Ten News time will be...*"

Cynthia took long and slow breaths as she looked out the window to Prince Street and West Broadway. Her mind went back to Myers in his blue suit, and it sent her mind further back to the first time her brown spotlight eyes fell upon him.

It was the previous summer, on a mild Saturday in July of 1981.

She had been making her rounds on the blacktop. She wheeled and glided on red rubber wheels from one piece of street to another with her headphones snugly pressed against her ears. The radio was always tuned to Disco 92 WKTU, her favorite station.

She had been doing this very same thing since the warmest days of April that year. When she did this she was free. Free from the neighborhood girls who raised their noses to her, the backstabbers, and the mean girls. Free also from the mangy creeps that hung around doorways and street corners or hunched over stoops. With the headphones on, she couldn't hear their comments, and on her wheels, they couldn't catch up to her. What started out as a painkiller, a way to purge her anxieties and fears, steadily morphed into a daily ritual Cynthia found she could not live without.

Then one day a glorious thing happened. She noticed her thighs no longer rubbed together as she walked.

Shocked, confused, and unsure, Cynthia stood in front of her mother's full-length mirror. Her legs, from calves to thighs, had become tight and muscular. Over time, she noticed, those obnoxious jeers from the neighborhood creeps also morphed. They became smiles, whistles, and even kind gestures like opening a storefront door for her. Even her old supposed girlfriends started to invite her to come to the clubs with them, but she didn't hang out with them much longer. Something besides her body had changed, too. Those old girlfriends— the ones that were now nice to her but used to be mean—seemed obsolete and boring to Cynthia.

On that Saturday morning in the middle of July 1981, Cynthia gracefully glided over a vast grid of blacktop west of Sixth Avenue from Canal to Houston that was virtually deserted on weekends. Saturdays and Sundays, it was like a ghost town, with almost no people and no cars. The scent of printer's ink that hung heavy in the air was the only sign that anything actually happened in that area during the workweek. It was her favorite private paradise that came out of her roller-skating.

Finally, after hours of skating, Cynthia made the last of her dazzling spins, pirouettes, twists, and turns for the day. A million times she skated past the animal clinic, a townhouse, but never paid it any attention. He filled up her eyes from a block away as she glided across Varick Street on her way home. A man, tall and blonde, was trying to hang a wooden sign by the window to the side of an entrance to the townhouse. He straddled a small wrought-iron fence. She glided by silently and peeked behind a tree as the man struggled not to fall flat on his face while trying to fit the sign in place. She hoped he wouldn't.

Anyone could have seen it coming, but her trance was so deep that Cynthia was surprised when he turned to look at her. He smiled brightly, and his blue eyes, she swore, lit up the street. In a self-conscious tizzy, she panicked and skated off with a bass drum pounding in her chest.

Twenty minutes passed as she sat on a park bench on Sixth Avenue with a heart that raced and a mind that reeled. She felt like she had spotted a unicorn, and Cynthia knew she had to do something fast before someone else moved in. Cautiously she skated by once more and hoped to see the beautiful man again, but he was gone. The sign was hung, the front door of the townhouse was shut, and the shades were drawn. She looked at the sign again. It was a wooden panel, painted white, that was chipped and peeled. In black letters it read, *Help Wanted*.

The very next morning she stood before the shut front door. Cynthia took a deep breath and pressed the doorbell.

The image faded as she finished her water. She sat by the sill for a moment, biting the inside of her lip. She assumed Myers had already fired her. She couldn't blame him. Still, she wanted to tell him she quit. She eyed the dial on the black rotary phone, picked the receiver, and spun out the clinic's number.

She got a busy signal.

CHAPTER 4

"OK. I'll see you in a little while." Myers quietly put the reception-desk phone back in its cradle as he watched the kitchen entrance down the hall. He had to get downtown to One Police Plaza, but he didn't want Lucchese to know. He opened the top drawer of the reception desk and took a white paper napkin from the wad Cynthia saved from takeout orders. He wrapped the broken fingernail in the napkin and put it back into his pocket and headed toward the kitchen.

As he stepped into the kitchen, he saw Lucchese seated at the wooden table with a steaming coffee mug in his hand. There was a pot of coffee, another mug, and an open bottle of whiskey on the table in front of him.

Lucchese looked up. "So what did the kid tell you?" He poured some coffee into the other mug and then filled it nearly to the top with the whiskey and slid the mug in Myers's direction.

Myers hesitated. He wanted the drink, but like always, his conscience told him not to. All he needed was the right reason to ignore his conscience. He put his hand into his pocket, felt the napkin that was wrapped around the nail he found. He sat down across from Lucchese and lifted the mug.

"Well?" Lucchese added.

"Something about a witch," Myers said, staring into mug.

Lucchese swatted his hand in dismissal. "He's high is what he is. I've known that Santalesa punk since before he could walk, and whatever he says, take my word for it, he's lying. That courtyard they were in is where all the hopheads, drunks, and bums around here go to score."

Myers mulled over what Lucchese said. "That's an interesting point."

"Yeah," Lucchese said as he crossed his arms over his chest with a nod.

"The only problem with it is that it begs the question of what you were doing there tonight." Myers looked back down into his mug as he asked the question, but knew he would have to look Lucchese in the eye for the truth. He hated having to ask the question because, for some reason, Myers felt sorry for Lucchese and even a little bit afraid of him. Even when Myers knew he was being lied to, he didn't have the heart to call the guy out on it.

For the briefest of moments, Lucchese looked like a deer caught in the headlights of an oncoming eighteen-wheeler. "Well, that's easy, Doc. See, I was only in the courtyard because I was there to do damage assessment. See, Betancourt—he's the guy that just bought the place for his paper company—he's having the place gutted, and the construction company complained that the hopheads been breaking in at night and stealing their tools and things. You know, so they can buy dope. Betancourt asked me to have a look around and do a little damage assessment, but Veronica…well, she heard something and she just took off. Now, as you know, she's a strong one…and fast, too. Mother of God, is she fast! But she's not too bright sometimes and…and I couldn't hold her and that's when I found those two. Now, I don't know if she's trained to sniff out drugs, but it's clear that's what she found."

Strange, Myers thought, because if the dog was looking for drugs, why didn't she go after Tommy? "I guess you're right," Myers said with a nod and took a long swig of his drink.

"So what do you want to do with them?" Lucchese asked as he refilled Myers's mug. "Hey, I got an idea, Doc. Why don't I take the sick one up to St. Vincent's for you? You've had a rough night with your black eye and all. The last thing you need is to babysit Tinker Bell *and* his junkie friend."

Myers was stone-faced. He eyed the black canvas bag by Lucchese's feet and wanted to know what was in it, but didn't ask because he was afraid in doing so he might tip his hand. "For the time being, I'll let the sick one sleep it off."

CHAPTER 5

Tommy came back into the animal clinic, walked down the hallway, and stood outside the closed office door for a moment. The light from the kitchen bathed his back as he faced the shut door. His hand turned the knob and the door creaked open with an irritating whine.

He quietly closed the door behind him, stepped over to the bed in the darkness, and took a seat on the edge of the bed.

He wanted to say something, but didn't know what. Deep inside there was a nagging that something had to come out, but he couldn't find the words. He waited on some angel of inspiration, someplace to start, some kind of ignition, but all he could do was stall. It was like waiting to throw up and not being able to. Finally, he said, "Where have you been for the past three days? You bolted after the show for that Van Tassel chick and missed the best party of your life."

Frank stared blankly at Tommy. What could he say? It wasn't like Tommy could ever understand. He looked away and rolled over to face the wall.

Tommy didn't know what to say. For the first time in his life, he actually felt shunned. After a few minutes, there wasn't anything else for him to do but to take a seat on the floor at the foot of the bed. With his back to the wall, he closed his eyes and pressed his forehead to his knees.

Chapter 6

"**So Bob Wooten** says to me—with a straight face, mind you—'Do you remember that time I farted?' And I'm like, '*Which* time? There's a reason', I says, 'that we call you *Tootin' Wooten*, Bob.' It was all I could not to laugh in his face. He just stared up at me like a confused poodle before he finally busted out laughing." Auggie Winters, from the lobby of One Police Plaza, watched as a yellow taxi came to a halt in front of the main entrance steps of the New York Telephone building at 375 Pearl Street. He saw Myers step out. The door slammed shut, and as Myers whirled around the cab took off. "I have to go. Let me know about those Mets tickets." He hung up the wall extension phone.

Winters pushed open the glass door and stepped out into the heavy, humid air. Behind him, in the distance, he heard the hiss of light traffic on the Brooklyn Bridge. "Doc Myers!" he called out.

Winters was a fellow vet who worked for the NYPD Canine Division. They knew each other because Myers and Winters had worked together hand in hand with certain dogs at different times. At six five, he towered over most people, and as a result he tended to lean forward at a hunch. He had skinny arms and almost dainty wrists. Something about him always reminded Myers of a kid from his high school that would wear a suit everyday with white tennis shoes. Even though Myers knew Winters always wore leather shoes, he was always compelled to look.

"Auggie." Myers approached with an extended hand. "Can I buy you a drink?"

"Love to have one, but can't. Even lab geeks like me can't have a taste until my shift is over." He popped a cigarette into his mouth. He noticed Myers's black eye and made a questioning shrug.

Myers shook his head. "It's a long story."

"So then what's so important you came all the way down here at this hour?" He patted his chest pocket before he found a white book of matches.

Myers handed over the napkin wrapped around the long fingernail. "Can you tell me what this is?"

Winters looked it over. "It's a nail," he said flatly.

"I know that. I need to know what kind."

"Shouldn't you know? You're a vet."

"Let's just say I'd like a second opinion. Be careful, it's—"

"Whoa! That's sharp!" Winters sucked on his index finger with strained eyes as he gave it a second look. "I left my glasses upstairs, schmuck that I am." He held the nail up above his head, hoping to catch the light from the streetlamp the right way. It didn't help. "Even if I had my glasses, I couldn't tell you much, other than it looks like some kind of animal. My guess is a wolf maybe, but...I'd have to put it underneath a lens upstairs and scrape a sample from it before I could say for sure."

"How long will that take?"

"You in a rush?" He took out a pen and scribbled a phone number down on the inside of the matchbook. "Call me at this number in an hour."

As Winters watched Myers leave, his eyes panned to the right and fell on the sign over the bar. It read, *The Metropolitan.*

CHAPTER 7

"*...r eporting from the SoHo section of Manhattan where police are still searching for a Mr. Frank Balistrieri of Thompson Street. Police are looking for him in connection with the disappearance of Amy Van Tassel. Now, it's important to mention that the police have not identified Mr. Balistrieri as a suspect but want to speak...*"

Cynthia felt deflated as she stared at the telephone. She had come so close to finally igniting something with Myers, and then in a cloud of smoke it just disappeared. So much of her attention, her energy, and emotions had been invested with her feelings for Myers, now that it was over she didn't know what her next move would be. How would she feel in the morning? Probably like hell, and she dreaded having to deal with all the fallout. She knew already that she wouldn't be able to get out of bed, and then when she did finally drag herself from the bedroom, her mother would want to talk about it. She cringed at knowing the neighborhood gossips would have their comments.

For Cynthia, working with Myers was like leaving the farm and seeing Paris. Now that she had seen Paris, going back to the farm was not only going to be painful but downright pathetic. However, Cynthia did know one thing about dreading those emotions: anticipating them was as bad as dealing with them. At least when dealing with them, she knew there would be a light at the end of the tunnel.

She lifted the receiver and spun around the dial for the first digit. Some bitter feeling of not knowing what to say got the best of her and she hung up.

She threw caution to the wind and spun out all the seven digits. The numbers dialed sounded like muffled machine gunfire in her ear. For a moment, there was a silence that hung in midair.

Finally, it started ringing. One ring became two and then a third and a fourth. After the ninth ring she bit the inside of her mouth in anticipation. The phone rang fifteen times in total.

"C'mon! Put the down the sauce and answer the damn phone, you lush!" she hissed and slammed the phone down in its cradle. She stood, arms crossed, with a frown and a leg that twitched nervously. She stormed into her bedroom, threw on a white tank top and a pair of jeans, and pulled her hair back into a ponytail. She grabbed her keys off her dresser and started off in a huff down the stairs.

She was as quiet as a church bell and self-conscious as always.

CHAPTER 8

The phone's ringing hit Lucchese's last nerve. The long, tubular fluorescent light above the kitchen sink flickered and stuttered every few seconds as he sat alone at the table. The waterline on the bottle of whiskey opened earlier had dropped considerably since Myers had had retrieved it from the trash can earlier.

"You really are a toxin, aren't you?" The priest's voice was a cold whisper in Lucchese's ear. *"It makes sense when some people say that the best thing they ever did was join the Marines, but for you it was the only smart thing you ever did."*

"I didn't have much of a choice, now did I?" Lucchese searched the kitchen before finding the priest's image in the kitchen window. "No one in that courtroom was more surprised than me when he told me he was shipping me out Semper Fi. You worked out that arrangement. I'd have bet my life the judge would've put me away for at least five years for beating on a cop the way I did."

It was an annoying and nagging ring that grated on his nerves. It was the kind of ring that made a person want to answer the phone just so it would stop its nagging whine.

"Is he ever going to answer it?" he muttered. Why wouldn't Myers just answer it?

"I think you should answer it," the priest said.

"For the love of God!" He stormed out of the kitchen and headed down the hall to the reception desk. The blinking light on the phone grew bigger and brighter as he approached. His heavy hand reached and his sausage fingers wrapped around the receiver like a polar bear plunging into the water for a salmon.

Then it just stopped ringing.

"*Look,*" the priest said, lighting a cigarette. "*I'm not judging you. As far as I'm concerned, you did the right thing. Good riddance to bad people is my motto...the point is, DeMarco was holding that crap over your head for too long. Now that the stinky little meatball is out of the picture, there's really nothing holding you back now. Except...*"

He stood still and stared at the now quiet phone. He released his grip and walked back down the hall to the kitchen. He took his seat at the table again but faced the opposite direction and poured himself another drink.

Turning his back didn't help. He could still hear the priest's voice.

"*You understand that now you're going to have to kill that boy, don't you?*"

CHAPTER 9

The Metropolitan was a college bar that the students from Pace University would fill during the school year, but on a weeknight in the summer it was nearly empty. Myers sat alone at the end of the bar. He nursed a mug of Conquistador-brand beer from the tap while he picked at a bowl of paltry-looking peanuts. Being out of the clinic and away from Lucchese afforded him time to think. He looked at his reflection in a dingy mirror behind the bar and spotted a squalid-looking phone booth in the corner near the restrooms. He suddenly thought about Cynthia.

What a night it had been, too. Earlier, as he got ready for their date, he swore to himself up and down while he paced his bedroom that he was not—repeat, not—going to be a stiff.

He raised his arms in front of his bedroom mirror to see if any sweat rings had formed beneath his armpits. He struggled with the clasp on his watch. It sprang off his wrist three consecutive times, and the last time, as he cursed under his breath and picked it up, he smacked his head on the night table. He looked at the spot over his eye in the mirror. No bump, no bruise, but it stung pretty bad.

It's too hot in here, he thought.

Nervously he tied his necktie for the fifth time before he felt satisfied. He gently put on this jacket and was ready to go. His shoelaces were tied, his hair was combed, and his watch was on his wrist. He grabbed his keys off the dresser, walked past the mirror, and nearly choked.

He wasn't wearing any pants.

"Am I Teddy Kennedy now?" he blurted out as an arrow of anxiety pierced his chest. He stepped back and paced around like a decapitated chicken. He caught a glimpse of himself in the mirror. The tea bags had worked, and he no longer had those bags under his eyes.

Oh, God, he thought, *what if she wants to have sex?* She was going to want to have sex. His face dropped into his hands. *If she saw me like this,* he thought, *she wouldn't want to have sex.* He composed himself by taking a deep breath and standing up straight. He looked himself over in the mirror slowly. With the exception of not wearing any pants, he looked fine.

He closed his eyes and took a long deep breath. "The problem isn't sex, Myers," he said to himself. "The problem is that you haven't had sex sober since...ever." It was a real revelation for him. An epiphany almost. "I've never had sex sober. Not once. I can't drink around her because she hates it when I do, but I need to drink because she makes me nervous."

He thought it over for a few minutes when the answer finally came to him. "Myers, just do what you always do. Play it cool. I can't go wrong with that," he said with a smile as he reached for his pants.

As Myers sipped on his second beer, he couldn't stop thinking about the look on Cynthia's face just before she decked him. That image was burned into his memory. It hadn't been a look of anger, hate, or even frustration, but one of hurt and disbelief. As if all the wind had been taken out of her sails and she'd just then realized that she was stuck with absolutely nothing. All the happiness just drained from her. In Myers's mind, him getting off with just a black eye was him getting away with murder. He checked his watch and saw that it had been just a little over an hour since he stepped into the bar. He finished the rest of his beer and headed over to the phone booth.

"Play it cool..." he mocked as he closed the folding door of the phone booth. "I'll be sure to submit my application to MENSA now." He dropped a dime in the coin slot and spun out the number Winters had written down for him.

"Is this Myers?" an unfamiliar woman's husky voice asked from the other end after only one ring.

"Yes."

"There's a bit of a crisis going on. Winters wanted me to tell you that the results came back. It's human."

"Human? But—"

"He left the sample for you at the front desk in an envelope," she said curtly.

"Where's Winters? What's going on?"

"He was called away. Look, the brass is going hog wild around here to-night…" There was a pause and then her speech slowed and her tone softened. "I'm not supposed to tell you this, but they're grabbing every available cop to find some kid from Thompson Street."

CHAPTER 10

There it was again! That flyer with a sketch and the word *WANTED* written beneath it. Cynthia first saw it outside her building on the lamppost at the corner of Prince and West Broadway. She noticed it again where Prince crossed Thompson Street, and then it was all over lampposts, pinned beneath windshield-wiper blades of parked cars, and even stapled to trees.

Just a minute earlier, as Cynthia turned the corner at Thompson and Spring, she noticed up ahead a cluster of cops standing around two parked police cruisers by the uptown E-train entrance. Had she paid any attention and been less self-conscious, she would have seen the eyes of the male officers take a long, slow walk over her.

"*Mami*," someone called out.

Instinctively Cynthia rolled her eyes, and then realized it was a woman's voice and not a man's. She stopped and noticed for the first time since she left her house that there were cops everywhere and a Channel 7 News van was parked by the side of Thompson Park. She turned and saw a petite police sergeant approach.

"Have you seen this man?" Araya asked, holding the piece of paper.

Cynthia took the paper and looked at the picture. She recognized Frank's face from the neighborhood, but didn't really know him. Her eyes scanned the name from the sergeant's badge. "I'm not sure of the address." Cynthia thought it over. "He lives on Thompson Street—"

"Yes, we know where he lives," she cut in. "Have you seen him?"

"Not tonight, no." Cynthia felt as though the woman had snapped her head off.

"Hold on to that, please. If you do see him, call the number at the bottom." With that, the sergeant turned on her heels and walked off.

Cynthia stepped away but felt uneasy. Her exchange with the sergeant seemed odd. She didn't like having some cop's eyes burn into her. Also the way she called her *"mami"* put her off; like they were supposed to be friends. By the time she crossed Sixth Avenue the last thing on her mind was the flyer she tucked into her bag or Sergeant Araya. All she wanted to do was see Myers, tell him how she felt, pack her things, and be done with it.

CHAPTER 11

As Cynthia approached the townhouse, the first thing she noticed was that the front door was wide open. The screen door was closed, but the actual front door was not. She shook her head in frustration. "What's with this bozo? First he doesn't answer the phone and now this." She walked the four feet to the entrance and looked inside beyond the screen door and saw straight down the hallway to the illuminated kitchen. "Myers, you around?"

He's in the kitchen, she thought, *and he heard me, but he's ignoring me. He's ignoring me because he's mad at me. He's mad at me because I punched him in the face.*

She pulled open the screen door, stepped inside, and then stopped dead in her tracks. Some oppressive and horrible feeling hung in the air. With hesitation, she slowly walked to the reception desk and flipped on the wall light switch. The waiting area became washed in a soft white glow. She looked at the phone, the blotter on the desk, and her empty chair. It was hard to believe it was over. She'd started working with Myers shortly after he arrived in the city, and now she wondered how long it would take before his clients forgot her. It was hard to believe it had been a year.

But she wasn't there to reminisce. With a labored huff, she reluctantly walked down the hall. When she reached the kitchen entrance, she hesitated, mulled over what she planned to say, and stepped through. She felt like an idiot and twice as deflated when she saw only Lucchese seated at the kitchen table. His face was contorted with stress and one arm dangled listlessly at his side while his other arm rested on the table with a coffee mug in his hand. He looked like a mess, she thought, a beaten man whose days were numbered. He dug into his front pants pocket, and pulled out a betting slip.

"Never put a dollar down on a horse named Immortality," he said as he crumpled the paper and threw it on the floor.

Some wiseass remark dangled from the tip of her tongue, but she kept it to herself. Instead she sighed and asked, "Where's Myers?"

Lucchese lifted his mug, realized it was empty, and pushed it aside. He went straight for the bottle. "Honey, you remember what the old Italians around here used to say about crossing Sixth Avenue after the sun went down, don't you?" He didn't wait for an answer. "There was a reason. *They* knew like I knew." He took a long, sloppy swig off the bottle. With closed eyes, he leaned forward and raised his index finger. "She's out, and mark my words, honey, she's bringing hell with her."

She stared at him blankly for a moment and then rolled her eyes. "Don't call me honey," she said as she turned and walked back down the hallway to her desk. She picked up the empty wastepaper basket to use as a box for her things and put it on the desk.

As she opened the desk's top drawer a blackened figured filled up the doorway on the outside. Her heart dropped when she realized it was Myers.

"Can we talk?" he asked from the stoop.

"Sure." She closed the drawer and put her hand on her hip.

"I mean out here," he said and opened the screen door.

"Look, you don't have to worry about paying unemployment..." she said as she stepped outside.

"I wasn't even thinking about unemployment."

"...because I quit." Her eyelids were heavy as she looked at him.

"You quit?"

"Yes." She kicked out her hip again and put her hand back on it in a defensive stance.

"Look, I wasn't planning on—"

"It's alright, Myers."

"—firing you. I was—"

"I get it now. I never really did it for you and—"

"—going to apologize and ask you—"

"—I get that now." She crossed her arms.

"Didn't do it for me?" Was he about to be hoodwinked? "Didn't do it for me?" he repeated. *Lady, I have a heart attack every time you're around*, he thought.

The lights inside the townhouse dropped out. The lights came back on but only to about half their strength. "I think the heat's causing a brownout."

She rolled her eyes across his face to take in the black eye. *I popped him pretty good*, she thought and stifled a small laugh.

"I hope it's not a blackout," Myers said, watching the porch light.

"Don't even say that. I still remember the blackout of '77."

CHAPTER 12

The whine of the office door opening woke Tommy up. He had nodded off, but he didn't look up right away because he assumed it was only Myers and he wasn't in any rush to take Frank to the hospital.

He didn't hear any footsteps, only the labored and forced breathing of someone else in the room.

Tommy opened his eyes and squinted as his eyes adjusted. The light from the kitchen was shut out as he heard the office door close. The figure in the dark was too husky to be Myers. He reached for the lamp on the night table and turned it on.

Lucchese stood over Frank with a wooden mallet cocked in one arm as he pressed a pointed wooden stake to the kid's chest.

"What the fuck are you doing, Rubber?" Tommy sprang to his feet.

"For the love of God." Lucchese's heart nearly stopped. His face became flushed and red with busted embarrassment. "What're you doing here, Tinker Bell? I thought you went home already."

"What do you mean, what am *I* doing here? I'm waiting for Myers." Tommy was indignant and rose to the balls of his feet with his fists clenched at his sides. His eyes fell to something that looked like a heavy glass ashtray on the night table and he picked it up. "What're *you* doing here?"

Lucchese relaxed his posture. "Rosebud, pull your head out of your ass and take a look at your friend."

Tommy looked and saw that Frank's face had become gaunt and his body, somewhat ashen in color, had become sinewy and tight. He also noticed that Frank's fingernails had grown.

Lucchese eyed the ashtray in Tommy's hand. "What're you going to do with that?" He gently placed the mallet and stake down on the bed. He rubbed his hands together and then raised them.

"I'm going to throw it at your enormous head if you don't step away from him."

"That's assuming you can hit me with it."

"You're kind of hard to miss."

They began to circle each other around a small coffee table in the center of the room. They never took their eyes off each other.

"You're going to have to throw it, Rosebud; you realize that, don't you?" Lucchese flinched only slightly as Tommy faked a throw. "I've seen you throw. Just like a girl, too."

"Yeah, yeah, keep talking, mongoloid," Tommy sneered.

With that, Lucchese charged forward and lunged. Tommy, in a fit of panic, shrieked like a cat, jumped up as if electrocuted, and ran around to the other side of the coffee table.

Lucchese huffed and puffed in frustration as Tommy still held the ashtray. "Rosebud!" Lucchese barked. "Step aside or I swear to God I'll break you in two."

"I'm not letting you hurt him!" Tommy shouted as he positioned himself between Frank and Lucchese. The ashtray was cocked and loaded in his hand.

Chapter 13

A loud sound of crashing roared down the hallway, out the front door of the town-house, and into Cynthia's and Myers's ears. Their heads both spun in the direction of the hallway.

They heard shouting from inside.

Myers looked at Cynthia and they read each other's thoughts. He opened the screen door and she followed him inside. The shouting grew louder as they walked down the hallway, and as they stood outside the closed door they both heard that it was Lucchese. Myers could feel Cynthia's breath on his neck and he caught a fading sample of the perfume she wore earlier that night.

Cynthia looked at Myers with a questioning expression.

"He's yelling at a neighborhood kid," Myers whispered.

Cynthia sighed, sidestepped Myers, and pushed the door open. Her jaw dropped at what she saw.

The entire office was a wreck, as if Myers had hired fate or a wind tunnel to be his interior decorator. The legs had been broken off one end of the coffee table so that it resembled a kid's bicycle ramp. One of Myers's floor lamps was laid on the floor with its decapitated shade off somewhere in a corner. The table fan Myers had brought in earlier was knocked over on the floor along with every piece of paper from his desk. The window blind dangled by a single hook, and the curtains had been ripped off the rod. A jagged and diagonal hunk of window glass swayed, then dangled, and finally fell with a crash into the back lot as if to say that was the final word.

In the center of the room, Lucchese whirled around in a rage with a stake and mallet raised. Tommy stood by the couch with Myers's wooden desk chair raised at Lucchese in defense like a lion tamer. They stared each other down as they caught their breath.

Myers was at a loss for words. His mouth moved, but no words came out. The scene before him was ridiculous. In the middle of the room was a veteran street fighter—a retired cop for crying out loud—out of breath with a flushed face while a tall and thin long-haired teenager held a chair. They were both surrounded by wreckage—collateral damage—which neither seemed to notice or care about.

Cynthia stepped around some of the debris as she entered the office, and she felt like she was visiting the site of a plane crash. "Holy shit," she said with equal parts chuckle and awe. She knew Tommy the same way Tommy knew her: from the neighborhood. They might have never even so much as spoken to each other, but they knew of each other.

The lights then stuttered and went out again. As the lights returned, they all jumped, startled by Veronica's sudden violent barking. The dog's violent shrieks were so loud that Myers, Cynthia, and Lucchese bolted from the office. The three of them shot down the hallway. Myers took the stairs two at a time with Cynthia on his heels.

As they entered the kennel, Myers took a swipe at the light switch on the wall and the room became drenched in a near-blinding fluorescent white light. Myers stepped into the kennel and over to Veronica, who lunged and rallied in her cage. Her barking was enough to make him deaf. Myers's usual use of soothing words and his gentle disposition failed to calm her.

Cynthia hung back in the doorway and watched as Myers and Lucchese tried to understand what upset Veronica. Her skin crawled and her mouth dropped as she watched a black shadow move away, like a fat cockroach that doesn't want to be seen, from the center of the floor beneath Myers's feet to a corner. Cynthia shifted out of the doorway into the kennel and pressed her back against the wall as the shadow moved across the floor to the door.

"Myers!" she yelled, never taking her eyes off the moving shadow as it hissed and then blew past her and out into the hallway.

Myers raised the locking pin on Veronica's cage and was shoved out of the way as the dog launched out of the cage in a dive. She hit the floor running, slipped on the surface, and kept moving.

"Did you see that?" Cynthia asked Myers and Lucchese. "Did you see that thing?"

"See what? What thing?" Myers asked, heading out the doorway.

Cynthia looked at Lucchese, but he looked down and away as he walked past her.

The three of them ran down the stairs. Myers's feet hit the last step first. He skidded on the area rug and then ran straight to his office. Cynthia had passed Lucchese at the top of the stairs and was on Myers's heels again. She slammed into his back as he stopped short outside the office.

Inside the office, Tommy stood where they left him. Veronica held a firm position and faced him with taut muscles that flexed and flared with each bark she spit out. Moving only his eyes, he saw Myers. "I hate this dog," he said with a crack in his voice.

Myers stepped inside the office slowly as he eyed the dog's one hundred and fifteen pounds of muscle that stood before Tommy. For some reason Veronica did not like Tommy, but he knew if he could just grab hold of the leather collar around her neck he could calm her down.

Cynthia saw it again. "Myers," she said with a pointed finger at the nasty black shadow that clung to a corner in the room where two walls and the ceiling met. It jiggled and writhed like a pus-filled sack about to drop, and Cynthia cringed in both fear and disgust.

From his crouched position, Myers looked back at her, annoyed. He saw her extended digit and the look of horror on her face. His head and eyes traced the path of her finger, and his own jaw hit the floor as he saw it. Then it made sense: Veronica wasn't barking at Tommy, but at the shadow in the corner.

Veronica inched forward and without warning broke out into a new fit of shrieking wails that Myers felt in his bones. A terrible feeling swelled in the pit of his stomach as he watched Veronica slowly step closer to the corner. She moved past Tommy, and then in one move, she leapt forward.

The shadow in the corner shot forward, hit the floor, and spread out in a black puddle. The puddle then recoiled, and sprang up from the floor like a geyser. The black mass reshaped to become the torso of a woman that rose with the shadow as its vapor trail and loomed over them. She hung above, scanned the room, and then dropped back to the floor as an oily sack.

Horrified, Myers shouted and tried to grab hold of Veronica's collar but missed as she lunged forward. The shadow rose up from behind her and silently took the full form of a woman with long, flowing near black hair and wrists adorned with lopsided rows of bangle bracelets. Veronica was never aware of what was behind her. In one quick movement, she was hoisted off the floor by the fur between her shoulder blades.

The woman turned to face them as Veronica dangled from her left hand. She moved closer and spread the fingers of her right hand like a fan. Nails like daggers stretched from the fingertips, and Myers noticed then that the nail of the middle finger was missing. Veronica squirmed and snapped, but the woman's strength was uncanny.

The woman's vibrant green eyes locked onto Lucchese's eyes as she pressed the nail of her index finger to Veronica's throat. In one quick and smooth movement, she slid the nail from the left to the right.

For a moment, nothing seemed to happen, and then Veronica's body hung in midair and fell to the floor, headless.

They all gasped. Tommy turned his head out of fear and disgust. He collapsed on one knee and threw up.

A knot twisted in Lucchese's stomach from where all the wind had been sucked out. Suddenly a rage boiled up in him. He raised the stake and lunged forward at the woman, but stopped dead in his track as her hand seized his throat.

Cynthia stared wide-eyed as she watched Lucchese's feet lifted off the floor as a devious smile grew on the woman's face. Her grip constricted. Lucchese's feet kicked, and he dropped the instruments from his hands to clutch her wrist.

On the bed Frank stirred and then moaned. The woman looked down at him, and the demented expression on her face was overcome by a saddened one.

She released her grip. "Soon," she hissed, and she slammed Veronica's head into Lucchese's gut as he fell to the floor. She sat on the edge of the bed and took Frank into her arms.

Tommy gibbered and shook in his curled position on the floor where he pressed himself into a corner between the couch and the wall. With one eye open, he saw the woman lift and hold Frank's head. She held him close by pressing her palms against his shoulder blades. Then she brushed away her hair from her right shoulder and pressed her neck to Frank's mouth and her mouth to his neck..

For nearly a minute Myers, Cynthia, and Tommy watched as a glimmer of life sparked within Frank. Only Lucchese, who sat on his heels and held the lifeless and blank-eyed face of his friend to his chest, didn't pay attention. His own slack-jawed expression matched the one he held in his hands.

The woman broke away from Frank and rose. Her eyes scanned the faces in the room and then burned a stare into Tommy. "Now I'll take what I've come for!"

Tommy scrambled and tried to grab Frank's ankle, but Frank pulled away from his friend and shunned Tommy's help.

With a wave of the woman's hand, the entire room became drenched in a cold and absolute darkness that none of them had ever experienced. They could see nothing and only feel the chilling frigidity about them. As if the entire world—all of existence—and their eyesight had been erased.

Like sunlight breaking and stretching through holes and cracks of a cloudy fog, the blackness disintegrated and they saw that the woman was gone.

Instinctively, Tommy's eyes fell to the cot. It was empty.

Chapter 14

"Did you see that?" Myers stewed as he paced the kitchen floor. He wanted to scream and rip Lucchese's head off. "What was that?" He took two long, exaggerated strides—lunges, really—at a time, then turned and did the same thing in the opposite direction. "She...*It* knows Lucchese. Did you hear what she said?"

Cynthia thought she smelled gasoline. Then her thoughts went to Veronica, and the vivid and graphic scene replayed in her mind. No matter how hard she tried, she couldn't shake it. "Poor dog," she said.

Myers stopped his pacing and dropped to a chair next to her at the kitchen table. He ran his hands through his hair and then dropped his face into them. "What do you know about Lucchese?"

"What, like how well do I know him?"

"Yeah, sure," he answered with an eager nod and anxiously eyed the closed office door.

"Not well," she said. "I mean, I only know the rumor that he watched his own father murder his mother."

"No wonder he's so messed up."

"The story goes that he watched his old man cut her heart out when he was like four or five. The cops never caught his father. After that the priests and nuns took him in and he was raised in St. Anthony's."

"Anything else?"

"He's a retired cop, but people say he was thrown off the force. I've heard he's a mob enforcer...that he gets rid of people for Charlie DeMarco."

"Gets rid of people? Like a hit man?"

"I mean like he's muscle for hire. A lot of people say he's in for a lot of money with Charlie DeMarco and that DeMarco owns him..." The image of Veronica replayed in her mind again. "There's something else, too. Some people have always said that his name isn't really Lucchese and that he's not even Italian."

Myers gnawed on his thumbnail. "I'm starting to think he's not exactly on the level with me."

"You're just *starting* to think that?" She was amazed. "Myers, he's full of shit. Don't believe a single word that comes out of his mouth. He mixes up the truth within a lie so you don't know which one is which. He's a bad guy. I think you're the only person around here that doesn't realize it, and he knows that you don't, which is why he's latched onto you. You're too nice. If you actually think that guy is your friend..." Something on the floor by her foot caught her eye. It was Lucchese's open black canvas bag. She leaned down, picked it up, and put it on the table. Her eyes widened at what she saw inside. "Myers, I think there's a lot more than what Lucchese's told you."

Myers leaned over and peeked inside the bag. He reached inside and lifted out one of many quart-size bottles that were capped tightly. Inside the bag were long strips of shredded rags. Myers held the bottle. He uncapped it, took a whiff, and turned his head away. "It's a Molotov cocktail."

"Was he planning on washing dishes afterwards?" Cynthia asked as she took a bottle of green dishwashing liquid from the bag.

"He's making poor man's napalm." Myers put the bottle back in the bag. "I don't get it, Cynthia. How do you burn down a brick building?"

She mulled it over. "Maybe not burn it down, but burn up everything inside of it. You know, like an oven."

"This night just keeps getting weirder and weirder." Myers dug into his front pocket and took out the envelope Winters left for him at front desk of One Police Plaza. He took out the fingernail and put it on the table. "I found this stuffed beneath Veronica's collar earlier. It came off that thing that was in there. I had a friend of mine analyze it at the lab. He says it's human."

The muffled sound of the flushing toilet reminded Myers that Tommy had locked himself in the bathroom.

"And do you know anything about this *witch* story the kid told me about earlier?" he asked, barely above a whisper.

She cocked an eyebrow and cracked a smile. "I haven't thought about that story in years. They used to tell it to us when we were kids…"

"Who told you?"

"The adults," she said with a shrug of her shoulders. "It was a stupid story the adults used to tell you to be good. 'If you're bad the witch will come for you,' or 'if you don't listen to your parents the witch will get you'…that kind of thing." Cynthia's mind drifted. "Except…"

"Except what?"

"Well, I remember some of the old people…they had a different spin on it." She eyed the closed office door. "Most of the people talked about it like a ghost story, you know. They'd sit around talking about it and you'd get goose bumps all over, but you'd forget about it in an hour. But some of the old people didn't even want to talk about it. If they heard you mention the witch they'd make the sign of the cross and shun you like you were a leper, but a lot of them actually felt bad for her because her whole story was so sad."

"Her story?" Myers's eyes bulged in disbelief. "What is it?"

"It's a story, mind you," she said with a shrug of her shoulders as she adjusted the band around her ponytail. "She became that way because of love. She was in love with a Spaniard who was sort of like a sorcerer or occult master or something."

"Occult master?" Myers's normal instinct to roll his eyes waned.

"Like a magician, I think. I don't know all the details—nobody does—but he used her as a decoy to trap a vampire in a village somewhere back in Spain, only she ended up getting bitten before he could kill the vampire. Then he turned his back on her, married some other woman, and came here. Then she followed him here and the Spaniard, with a priest from St. Anthony's, used a spell or holy water or whatever to keep her trapped in that building for the past fifty years."

"What happened to the Spaniard?"

"No idea. It's a story, Myers; that's all I know."

Myers rubbed his chin in thought. He would have laughed in Cynthia's face if she had told him that story earlier in the evening, but after what he had seen he wasn't so sure anymore.

Cynthia swatted her hand in a tiff and opened her bag. "That's only one problem, Myers. Every cop in the city is looking for those two right now." She unfolded the flyer and handed it to him.

As Myers entered the office, he half expected to see Lucchese still on the floor sitting on his heels. He didn't expect to see Lucchese on his knees as he rolled Veronica's body up in a white sheet from the cot.

"I need a garbage bag." Lucchese stood up, walked past Myers and out of the office.

Myers noticed that Lucchese used the pillowcase to put Veronica's head in and was startled as Lucchese stormed back into the office with a handful of black garbage bags that flapped in his wake. He dropped to his knees and stuffed one end of the body into the black plastic and then then did the same at the other end. He put the head in another bag and tied the remainder of the bag into a knot.

Lucchese lifted the body and held it across his two open arms. "You mind getting that other piece for me?"

"Sure," Myers said absently.

"I need a shovel, Doc. Do you have one?"

"A shovel? Where are you planning on burying her?"

"I don't know," he said, looking away. "Somewhere...anywhere."

"You need to think this through."

Lucchese sidestepped Myers and walked out of the office.

Myers stepped out of the office. "You can't go out like that. You're covered in blood, Al, and there's a million cops on the other side of Sixth Avenue." Myers ran up behind him. "What're you going to do, bury her in Central Park and think no one will see you?"

"If you're smart, Doc, you'll come with me." He reached the screen door.

"What I'm trying to tell you is that I have a better way of doing this."

Lucchese stopped. He turned his head with an eyebrow raised inquisitively. "I'm listening."

Chapter 15

Myers and Cynthia stood at the tail end of a yellow cab and together slammed the trunk shut. Lucchese waited in the backseat.

She handed Myers a white envelope. "I spoke to Dr. Byrne and everything is arranged. He'll meet you at the back entrance on Ninety-Sixth Street."

"Whatever you do, don't let the kid leave until we get back." Myers peeked inside the envelope. "Thank you," he said as he touched her forearm. "I really appreciate this."

She rolled slightly on the balls of her feet and looked down. She felt his hand touch the back of her head and then he pressed his mouth against hers. It was a short and tongueless kiss, but it was warm and genuine. She nearly lost her breath.

He opened the cab door. "Don't quit on…this…me. Don't quit on me," he said as he got into the cab and then drove away.

CHAPTER 16

Nearly an hour passed and the office didn't look half bad. Cynthia stood with her hands on her hips and blew back a strand of hair that fell over her left eye. She had picked up all the pieces of broken glass, reattached the window blind, picked up the fallen lamp. The broken coffee table was beyond repair, and she had put it outside in the back lot where Myers kept the garbage. She had cleaned all of Veronica's blood off the floor.

Tommy appeared in the doorway and looked at her blankly. He rubbed one eye while he held up his beat-up and dingy pair of Pro-Keds at his side. His black T-shirt was flung over his shoulder, and the waist button of his jeans was undone.

Just looking at him made her feel fat; he had no extra body fat to speak of. She shot him an incredulous expression.

An unlit cigarette dangled from his lips. "What?"

She gestured to the vomit on the floor.

"C'mon, you're kidding, right? I'm not touching *that*." He placed his palm on his stomach and took a step back.

"No, you're right, Tommy. Just let me go down the hall and get my magic wand. It's not like I didn't do everything else already while you were puking or taking a nap." She caught herself and paused. "It's only going to take two minutes. The sooner you get it done, the sooner you can go back to the bathroom and do whatever it is you do in there."

He didn't know if she was serious or making fun of him. "Can I smoke a cigarette first?"

She clicked her tongue and rolled her eyes.

Chapter 17

Cynthia sat in her chair, elbows on the desk, and rubbed her temples with her eyes closed. What a day it had been. She just wanted to go home and crawl into her bed.

The screen door swung open and snapped shut with a bang.

"So, me and my friends got this band. You know, Moe and Frank," Tommy said. "I know you know Moe, right? He's short with long black hai—"

Without looking up, she raised one palm. "I've read the papers."

He stepped around the desk so that he stood behind her. Looking over her shoulder, he said, "Anyway, we got this record deal and we're going to make a record pretty soon…" He paused and waited for her to say something. When she didn't, he put his hands on her shoulders and gently caressed her. "So, what does that do for you? You feel like sitting with me on the couch?"

"You feel like getting smacked?" she asked, raising her head.

He went around to the other side of the desk, paced back and forth, and then walked into Myers's office. A minute or two later he came back out with a stack of records and plopped down on the waiting-room couch. With the stack of records on his knees, he looked at them one by one and commented. "Tony Orlando and Dawn, Carly Simon…and…ewww…James Taylor. Is Myers lame or what?" Tommy nearly choked when he came across the *Saturday Night Fever* soundtrack. "I'd pay real money to see Myers do the Hustle."

Cynthia watched him as he stood up and walked with the records back into Myers's office. She really wanted to smack him. She wanted to stand up, call to him, and when he would turn to her with that glazed-over and vapid expression on his face, she would pelt him across the head with an open but firm hand. *Heat wave or no heat,* she thought, *this jerk needs to show some respect.*

When Tommy came over to her desk again he didn't say anything but flashed his smile at her. She figured it must work wonders with girls his age. He was hot; there was no point in denying it. Younger, hot, but so annoying.

"I'm bored," he sighed with eyes that didn't make contact with hers, but that wandered, lost.

"Then go do something."

"Like what?" he moaned.

"I don't know. Go finish cleaning up Myers's office. Just stop bothering me. Shoo!"

He stared at her blankly. "But I don't want to clean Myers's office."

"Why?"

"I don't know." He shifted his weight from one leg to another. "I just don't feel like it."

He muttered something as she flopped back down on the couch. He popped a cigarette in his mouth. "You got a match or anything? I can't find my lighter."

Yeah, I got a match for you. Your face and my... She opened the top drawer and pulled out a white book of matches. Without looking at him, she flipped the matches over to him.

He leaned down and picked up the matches by his foot. "I like your buck-teeth," he said.

"I don't have buckteeth."

"Yeah," he said, almost laughing. "You do."

"No, I don't."

"They're slightly buck." He stood up, ran his hands through his hair, and leaned over the desk.

She could feel his eyes burning a hole in her cleavage. She looked up. "I have a slight overbite." She frowned for a second and then a lightbulb went off over her head. "Hey, I bet you're in the mood for an egg cream. I know I'm really in the mood for an egg cream. Why don't you go into the kitchen and make us some?"

"What am I, ten? No." He threw his hands up in the air. "Cut me some slack, woman!"

She nearly laughed in his face. "I realize it's hot in here, and God knows, you're bored. There's not a lot I can do for you. So why don't you wait for Myers to come back without being a pain in my ass?"

"How long's that going to be?" he whined. "I've got things to do. In case you weren't listening, me, Moe, and Frank got a record deal. We have important people to meet, things to do…"

She suddenly didn't feel like laughing anymore. "Tommy, we're all feeling a little weird right now. What happened was—"

"She stole my friend!"

She shot up and put one hand on her hip. "That's what I was wondering, Tommy. Is it your friend you're worried about or the fact that he's your ticket out of here?"

At first his mouth made little jerky movements, but no sound came out. "If you only knew half as much as you want people to think you do…" He made a quick gesture, looked as if he might spit in her face or start crying, and then stormed off down the hallway.

Tommy slammed the kitchen door shut and stood with clenched fists. He breathed heavily and wanted to break something. He swung open every cabinet door and cupboard. He flipped on the faucet, pounded his fists on the counter-top. Tommy turned around, noticed the pantry doors, and opened them. The shelves, floor up, were stocked flush. He saw several jars of his own sauce in the jars he packed for Vinny Sr. with the same labels from the pizzeria.

He reached for a jar, held it and it up, and saw a small sticker tag from Paladino's with a *$4.00* price stamped on it. "That rat bastard," he hissed as he put it back on the shelf.

His eyes wandered around the kitchen where they came across a small wine rack and a refrigerator. He opened the refrigerator and saw it was well stocked.

CHAPTER 18

Lucchese waited for Myers and nursed a bottle of bourbon dressed in a brown paper bag while he leaned against a streetlamp outside a liquor store at the corner of Second Avenue and Ninety-Third Street. He saw Myers come out of the back entrance of the NYC Animal Care Facility. The expression on his face said he carried the weight of the world on his shoulders.

"They'll send her ashes to me in a few days," Myers said and reached for the bottle and took a healthy swig. "I need you to come clean. We both know there's more to all this than you're telling me. That thing—whatever it was—knows you."

Lucchese nodded. "Sure, sure; because she…it spotted me in the courtyard earlier."

"When you were doing damage assessment?" Myers asked flatly.

"That's right."

"He doesn't believe you," Lucchese heard the priest mock.

Here goes, Myers thought and sipped hard on the bottle. "What were you *really* doing there? You can smoke-and-mirror this story all you want, but we both know you're full of shit, Al. I saw what's in your duffel bag. Who does damage assessment with homemade napalm?"

Lucchese made a bitter face and snatched the bottle. "For years, God knows how many, there's been rumors that's there's gold hidden in that place, but there's not. The problem is you can't tell any of *these* people that."

"What people?"

"Charlie DeMarco."

"What does he have to do with any of this?"

"It's no secret that I racked up some nasty debts playing the ponies, Doc. I'm in for a lot of money to DeMarco, but he tells me that if I assist him, his jerk-off son and retard nephew break into that place before the demolition crew does, he'll wipe my slate clean. The catch is that once they were out, with or without the gold, I was to torch the place."

He wraps up the truth within a lie so you don't know which is which, he heard Cynthia's voice echo in his head. "What happened?" he asked apprehensively.

"What do you think happened, Doc? They went in there and…" Lucchese shrugged his shoulders.

"And what?"

He bit his bottom lip. "They didn't come out."

It worked out well for you, Al, Myers thought. "What about the kid?"

"What about him?" Lucchese asked as he began to walk away.

"We have to go get him," Myers said and grabbed Lucchese's forearm in desperation without thinking. "You're the one person who can actually do something and you're just going to let the kid disappear? It's like watching a lamb go off to slaughter."

"It's really in your best interest to kill him." The priest patted Lucchese on the shoulder.

In one swift move, Myers's arm was thrown back and his body was spun around with his face pressed up against the coarse brick wall of the liquor store. His legs were spread and his arm was twisted behind his back in a painful chicken wing. He felt Lucchese's elbow pressed into the back of his head.

Lucchese spewed out a garble of words in a nasty tone that threatened Myers for putting his hands on him. Then he said, "Are you nuts, Doc? We all just got made by the Angel of Death. If you think I'm going anywhere near that place, you're crazy."

After a minute, he released the pressure. Turning around to face him, Myers saw Lucchese's face mangled with rage. In a flash, it changed back.

"Hey, hey, no foul no harm, right?" Lucchese said in a soothing voice as he patted Myers's shoulders and straightened out the shirt he rumpled. "What do you say, we both hit that after-hours joint down on Warren Street? I'm sure they still got a card game going."

Myers was beside himself and at a loss for words, but stepped back and away. He just stared at Lucchese in disbelief and watched a yellow cab from the corner of his eye. Suddenly he didn't see Lucchese as a misunderstood frump, but as the asshole everyone else saw. As if guided by some unseen force, Myers raised his hand and flagged down the cab.

"Cynthia was right about you," Myers said as he reached for the door handle. "You really are a bad guy."

The door slammed and the cab drove off.

Now it was Lucchese who was at a loss for words and beside himself. He stood at the corner and watched the cab's taillights fade away down Second Avenue.

CHAPTER 19

The aroma from the stove slipped beneath the shut kitchen door, floated down the hallway, and hovered over Cynthia's desk. It slowly formed an invisible hook and grabbed her by the nose. Her stomach grumbled and it was at that moment that she realized she hadn't eaten since her date.

She stood up, stretched with an arch of her back, and let out a long and labored yawn.

As she walked down the hallway to the kitchen, the radio playing grew louder. A song was just ending as she opened the door.

"You're listening to WPLJ 95.5 FM, the place where rock lives. I'm Pat St. John and we're in the midst of a PLJ sixty-minute commercial-free Rock Block. Now something from the Stones. From '73's Goats Head Soup album, here's 'Doo Doo Doo Doo Doo (Heartbreaker)'..."

The music had already started as the DJ finished talking. Her silver-dollar-sized brown eyes twinkled and gently closed as her nose was filled with the intoxicating scent. Tommy was at the stove with his back to her. Her eyes followed his apron strings that crossed his back, around his neck and waist. He mumbled between singing along to the song on the radio. A glass of red wine stood on the counter to his left. He reached for it and pushed aside an open loaf of white bread in disgust.

Her eyes scanned the room. She saw three pots and a frying pan on the stove. The pots steamed, bubbled, and simmered. On the island in the kitchen's center was a large mixing bowl and large kitchen knife. Different vegetables were piled on the white marble top.

It all felt like a movie she had seen as a child, but instead of a mad scientist in a room filled with beakers and cauldrons, it was the nineteen-year-old pain in her ass in a living and breathing kitchen. When her eyes completed the tour of the kitchen that she had never, ever seen Myers use, she looked at Tommy as he leaned against the sink with his eyes fixed on her.

His finger gently lowered the volume of the radio. "Who would have thought a white-bread like Myers would have all this?"

"The Paladinos sent over a huge shipment because Myers took such good care of Nona Paladino's cat when it broke its leg, but that's only half of it. The rest comes from every widow or old lady in the neighborhood." She looked around again, amazed that Tommy could orchestrate so much. The entire kitchen was in a state of production with every vital piece of equipment performing a task.

He poured a glass of wine and handed it to her. "What do you see in him anyway? He's the type of guy that gets out of the shower to take a piss."

Taking it from his hand, she rounded the island and stood next him at the stove so that she could peer into the pots. "For one, he's mature, Tommy. He's serious." She sipped her wine. "This is good."

He placed his glass down and turned his attention to the stove. He raised a closed lid, dipped a spoon inside. "You want serious?" he asked. "I got something real serious to put in your mouth."

Her face twisted into a pissed-off stare and she cocked her fist, ready to pelt him. "You're such a pig!" Her words were cut short as he slipped the spoon into her mouth.

"Shut up," he said.

Her eyes widened as her taste buds threw a party. "Wow," she said. "You made that?"

He nodded gently as he dabbed the corner of her mouth with a napkin.

Her eyes locked on the spoon in hope that it would come back. "Can I have some more?"

"No." He pointed to the door. "Out."

"But—"

"But nothing." He touched her shoulders and eased her gently toward the door. "It's bad luck for you to be in here. It's not ready yet."

In defeat, Cynthia backed out of the kitchen and headed back to her desk. She noticed a folded piece of paper on the couch across from her desk. She picked it up, unfolded it, and scanned the words. It was a brochure for the New York Culinary Institute. She saw that Tommy had filled out his name and address. The she noticed a small triangular object roughly the size of a quarter on the couch also. Its edges were rounded and worn. She picked it up, too.

CHAPTER 20

The kitchen door flew open. "Yo, Bruiser, your dinner's ready," Tommy said. He turned back inside, and the door slammed shut behind him.

She moved fast and sprang to her feet, grabbed the small triangular object and the brochure, and headed down the hall. As she opened the kitchen, she stopped in her tracks. An uneasy look crossed her face as she saw the lights were dimmed and two white candles flickered. For holders he used two empty beer bottles from the garbage can.

Tommy caught her look of apprehension and rolled his eyes. "Don't flatter yourself, Batista," he said. "This isn't a date. I put the candles out because the light in here sucks." He placed a bowl heaped with pasta drowned in a red sauce on the table.

As she took the seat at the place setting with a filled wineglass, a string of commercials came to an end and the DJ announced another song. All of her attention was drawn to a serving dish that hosted a vast amount of fried chicken cutlets and fried zucchini as she draped the cloth napkin across her lap. Tommy filled her plate with two cutlets and a large heap of pasta.

The pasta was lighter and softer than any she had ever had before. It practically melted in her mouth. "What is this?"

"Cavatelli." He became defensive. "Something wrong with it?"

She shook her nervously. "Not at all. It's excellent," she said eagerly with a full mouth.

"I think I used all his flour."

"He won't notice." She looked like a chipmunk with packed cheeks as her fork probed the plate. "Oh, I found these on the couch." She pushed the strange object and the brochure across the table. "What's that triangle thing?"

"It's a bass pick. It's fatter and thicker because bass strings are fatter than a guitar." He stared at it and frowned. "It's also the reason I'm getting tossed from the band."

"I don't get it," Cynthia said only half attentively. She tried her best to sound interested, but she had taken her first taste of cutlet and was already thinking about eating the next one.

"All the *really* good bass players use their fingers. They don't need a pick. Like Geddy Lee; he uses his fingers."

"Is that a person?" She tried her best to seem interested, but couldn't have cared less as she poked her fork into the cutlet.

"It's not important. What's important is that…" He shook his head in disbelief. "Do you have any idea how good Frank is on the guitar?"

She shook her head, her cheeks packed. "Just what I've read in the papers and heard in the neighborhood."

"He's like Mozart good. Fuck Eddie Van Halen, fuck Jimmy Page and Jimi Hendrix, and fuck, like, whoever…I mean, he's invented an entire new sound. Moe is nowhere near as good on the drums as Frank is on the guitar, and Moe, for the record, is an excellent drummer. He's a top-ranking drummer but doesn't have half of Frank's talent. That's how good Frank is. When you put them together it's genius because they work so well together. You can't just have any slug on a bass weighing them down."

"If you play the bass as well as you cook, you shouldn't have a problem."

"That's just it," he mumbled. "I don't."

Cynthia noticed that Tommy hadn't touched his plate, but his glass of wine was nearly drained. She watched as he stared at the floor, lost in his thoughts, and then robotically refilled his wineglass while he popped a cigarette into his mouth. He reached for the candle in front of him and lit it. Then he stood up and leaned against the kitchen sink. The window over the sink was raised, and he blew out each drag he took through the screen. She noticed the crucifix and the chain it hung from around his neck. He looked lost to her, as if his mind was no longer in the kitchen.

Something in the way Cynthia viewed him changed just then.

He had always struck her as being a goof. The kind of person you would never rely on. The way he would flop around the neighborhood, taking those long strides as he walked and how he always flashed that searchlight smile of his. Also the attention he brought on himself by always letting everyone know that he was the life of the party. It made her slightly jealous, too, because the younger girls all seemed to get a kick out of Tommy. They acted more like siblings than girlfriends, and it made Cynthia wonder if there was more to him than she had originally thought.

Tommy broke the silence. "I never got into this band to reinvent the wheel or to be the next Beethoven. That's Frank; not me."

"So what did you get into for?"

"For the girls mostly…to get Anne-Marie Mariani's attention. But really it was because the band was our little thing. Just Moe, Frank, and me. We were like a team."

"The three musketeers," she said.

He smiled at that.

"So let him be Beethoven then. You've got other talents, Tommy." She gestured at the food on the table.

Tommy made a face. "Cooking's got no teeth," he said as he took a long sip from his glass. "Anne-Marie's right. My only real talent is being a jealous wiseass. I hooked up Frank with that Van Tassel girl knowing she would dump him. If he hadn't been all hung on her, he never would've met that…vampire witch."

"Explain."

"Not that long ago we played a set to a packed crowd at this dump called Jimmy Byrne's out in Flushing. That was *the* show of our lives and it went off perfectly. We even got called back for an encore! No other band that played that night did an encore and there were like six or seven other bands on the bill that night. We didn't know what to play because we played all our original stuff, so at the last second—literally as we're stepping out on the stage—we played the best version of "Whole Lotta Rosie" by AC/DC. It was so unexpected, so perfect that the place went fuckin' nuts. And as we're playing and nailing it I look over at Frank and he's actually smiling. Like, he looked so happy, but I knew it wasn't because of the show but because he was going to see Van Tassel as soon as it was over."

Cynthia couldn't help but smile as she was caught up in Tommy's excitement of reliving that night.

"The audience was in our hands and we're all having the best time up there. Except for Frank. He couldn't get out of there fast enough because Van Tassel showed up earlier that day and told him to meet her. Who knows what she promised him. He should have been happy. That was his moment…I mean, being on stage playing music is what he's here for. All I know is that for the past six weeks, Frank's been about as much fun to be around as a piece of cardboard, but Van Tassel shows up one afternoon and he's in seventh heaven like he won the lottery."

"You can't blame yourself for that."

"I can if I knew it would end badly."

"Explain."

Tommy rolled his eyes in embarrassment. "It's no surprise around here that I've got a thing for Anne-Marie for the longest time and that I'd been trying to get her to come to one of our gigs for just as long. Anyway, she and Frank have always had this *thing* between them. I don't even know what you would call it really, but they have it. He casts a long shadow, Cynthia. I'm tall, but not tall enough not to get caught in it. I finally got Anne-Marie to come to one of our shows, and I figured if I could distract Frank then Anne-Marie and I could maybe get something going."

"And?"

"I knew Frank would go for Amy. I had met her a few other times through other people and she always asked about him." He gripped his hair at the sides of his head. "Why couldn't he just do what he needed to do and be over with it? He always falls so hard for these girls."

"Did anything ever happen between you and Anne-Marie?"

"That's the killer." He drained his glass. "Nothing, zip, nada, zero. I made my move and she wasn't having it." He untied his apron's strings, took it off, and draped it over the back of his chair. "This wine's making me sleepy. I think I'll take a little nap on Myers's cot."

She didn't know what to say as he walked past her and went out the kitchen door.

CHAPTER 21

"**Y**ou need to sleep." She reached out for him, but he pulled away and moved to the other end of the bed where he sat on its edge.

"You've done—" Frank said as he inched away.

"Horrible things. That's what you think, I know." She looked down at her hands in her lap. "You can't understand this now, but in time you will. Now, you must to sleep."

Frank knew she was right; all he wanted to do was lie down and go to bed, but fear kept him going. "That man...the one in the box that you talk to...he was your lover?"

"Once, yes."

"Is that what you're going to do to me?" he asked, looking at the floor.

"No, no, love." She reached out for him, but stopped short. "He was my lover before I became this way. I became *this* because of him. He used me as a decoy and then not only shunned me, but tried to kill me."

She could see that Frank had become slightly less tense. "With the help of a priest he kept me trapped here, but when the priest died so did the spell. With the spell broken I could leave this place and go wherever I chose, but then you called me."

"I *called* you?"

"Yes."

"I didn't call you."

"You did, love. With your music, and when I heard it I knew I had found my kindred spirit." She reached for his hand and he let her hold it. "There is so much more I have to show you, love, but now you must sleep. When you wake, it will be different."

Then he lay down on his back and was submerged into and swaddled by a warm darkness that lulled him to sleep.

CHAPTER 22

For the next fifteen minutes Cynthia sat in the in the flickering candlelight while she sipped her wine and picked at the food. The screen door shrieked open and slammed shut with a snapping sound. Hurrying footsteps peppered the hallway floor.

She turned in her chair and saw Myers as he came into the kitchen. He paused and looked around, bewildered by the scene.

She shook her head. "Hungry?"

Until she asked he didn't know he was hungry. He went to the cupboard and got himself a plate with a knife and fork. He took a seat and moved Tommy's setting out of the way. "I honestly think we should talk to the cops. I don't know how to get the kid back. I don't even know what to tell the cops," he said, piling his plate. "You were right about Lucchese." He took a forkful without looking at it and popped it into his mouth. "I'm not even certain of what I saw happen tonight."

"Where is he anyway?"

Myers shrugged. "I cut him loose at Ninety-Sixth Street." He gestured to the wineglass in her hand. She handed it over to him. He paused and took a decent look at the spread on the table. "You made all this?"

She shook her head. "Tommy did."

"Where is he?"

"He's taking a nap on your cot. "

Myers stood up and walked to his office. He opened the door, gently called Tommy's name. His hand slid along the wall and flicked the light switch on.

The cot was empty. He scanned the room but found no trace of Tommy. Something on the cot caught his eye and he stepped to it. Glimmering in the light like a tiny starburst was Tommy's elegant gold chain and crucifix with the bag of weed next to it.

Myers picked it up and turned to see Cynthia in the doorway.

"He took off?" she asked. She stared at the crucifix that dangled from Myers's hand. "Don't worry; I know where he went."

Part Three
La casa della strega

CHAPTER 1

On her back, hands folded and fingers interlocked across her stomach, she was as still as a corpse. Her hair had been neatly pulled back into a ponytail; her makeup—foundation, lipstick, mascara, and blush—had been applied perfectly. In stark contrast to her appearance were a pair of cotton exercise shorts and a concert T-shirt that was as crisp and pristine as she was.

She was not dead; she was literally lying in wait and growing impatient. She opened one eye and saw the red digital display on her nightstand clock. She knew not to get too upset because it was only a matter of time.

Anne-Marie knew the value of predictability. She also knew that Tommy, despite being unreliable, was as predictable as the atomic clock.

She was caught off her guard and jumped a little as the first pebble cracked off her second story window.

"Pssst!" he rang out from down in the courtyard below.

She waited and smiled.

As the second pebble bounced off the windowsill she readjusted herself and got ready.

Again, "Psssst!"

There was a gap in his calls and throws. As she waited, Anne-Marie couldn't help but wonder if he ran out of pebbles.

"Pssssssst!" And the third pebble followed.

"Three's a charm!" she exclaimed as she sprang to her feet.

She switched the lamp on her nightstand to the dimmest of settings, feigned a slow and drawn-out yawn to get into character, and then quickly draped a scowl across her face. Then she straightened the hem of her oversized T-shirt. Her ponytail swung and wagged from the back of her head.

After fully raising the window screen, Anne-Marie poked her head out. She eyed him suspiciously, pretended to be annoyed, and cleared her throat. "I'm surprised it took you this long." A satisfied, but short-lived smile grew on her face. "What do you want, Tommy Santalesa? It's very late."

She stuck her palm out of the window to see how heavy the rain was falling.

"Shhh! Keep it down, Anne. Last thing I need is your father waking up." He stood in the cul-de-sac underneath a fat and leafy tree branch.

"Oh, please," she scoffed, swatting her hand. "His days of chasing you are long gone. Besides, he's too old and he's got a bad knee."

Tommy's face blew up into a bright smile as he noticed the graphic on her T-shirt. "Hey, you're wearing the shirt I stole for you!"

"Bought!" she said. "Moe confessed that you bought it and made up the story about stealing it. Not that I ever believed you anyway. One thing's for sure, Tommy: you're a wiseass, but you're no badass." She tapped her fingernail on the windowsill in thought. "I assume you've come to gloat?"

He shook his head hastily and said, "I don't know what you're talking about. Look, just don't run away or close the window or anything. I thought about what we talked about earlier and, for what it's worth, you're right." He rubbed his stomach and made a sour face. The butterflies in his stomach gnawed to get out. *Guilt pangs*, he thought. "I hooked Frank up with that Van Tassel chick because I was getting jealous. I never thought anything would ever actually come out of it. Alright, so I said it. I'm jealous. You know, sometimes being his friend really sucks. 'Frank's this, and Frank's that, and he's so wonderful and a what a great guy he is,' they're always saying. And I can deal with it most of the time, but the thought of you and him…" He trailed off as he shook his head with a stare of pure regret. "God forbid I actually let anyone know I'm bothered by something." Nervously he popped a cigarette into his mouth and dug in his back pocket for his lighter.

"We never had anything, you know," she said.

He backed a step with his palms raised. "I don't want details. Not that it matters anymore."

"I think of him like a brother, you dope." She noticed the cigarette in his mouth and wanted one. "Don't be so cheap. Throw me one of those."

He flipped open the lid and tossed one up to her. She caught the cigarette in her dainty and cupped hands. She placed it in her mouth and waited. She watched as he smoked his, deep in thought. Finally she said, "It's not like it's going to light itself."

Frowning, he reached for his lighter and threw it up to her.

She cracked its lid and lit the cigarette. Inhaling, she said, "What do you mean it doesn't matter anymore? I don't like the sound of that." Her hand popped open and the lighter fell down to his waiting hands.

"It means…" Tommy started, not quite sure of himself. "It means, maybe I'm finally growing up and I want to set things straight. Look, I only came here because I know you have a weird…I mean good relationship with…" He pointed his index finger to the sky. "You know, Him. Everybody knows you're a Jesus groupie."

"What's it you?" She became defensive.

"If you're still writing love letters to Christ in that little diary like you used to, I was thinking maybe you could put in a good word for me." He slowed down, backed up, and gave it some thought. "What I'm trying to say is—"

"How do you know I already haven't?" As she looked at him, it dawned on her that she had never seen Tommy this way before. He actually appeared tormented. "I'm not the one you should be confessing to, Tommy. Maybe you should talk to a priest."

He shook his head. "With all the changes in the parish lately? No. It takes time to develop a relationship, and besides, I like my penance tailored. You already know what a dope I am." He stood below her, nervously rubbing his stomach, shaking his knee, and taking one long drag on his cigarette after another. His eye caught her chest, and he noticed something was missing. She wasn't wearing the ankle bracelet. "Where's the dog collar?"

"As if you didn't already know."

"Know what?"

"Go on; play stupid. We both know the word's out that I broke up with Nicky tonight."

"Oh, yeah? You ditched the Bat?" His face broke into a smile and then he quickly suppressed it. "I mean, that really sucks, Anne. How come?"

"It's not important. But…" She threw her head back and laughed. "I figured out what IROC stands for. It fits Nicky perfectly." She ran her tongue along her two front teeth. "We're talking about you. Not me."

While she waited for him to respond, Anne-Marie finished what she wanted of her cigarette and stamped it out on the windowsill.

He shrugged his shoulders. "I thought about what you said. You know, about me and Frank, and you're right. Some of my comments about him weren't all that—"

"Some?" Her eyes spread out wide in disbelief.

In a fluster, he blurted, "Everyone around here acts like I'm supposed to name my firstborn after him—"

"It's a start!"

"But that's not the point…the point is who am I to say anything? I get that now." Looking away, he rubbed his chin. "I haven't been all that good to him a lot of the time. It's not that I wanted to hurt him, but…"

"I know."

"I just wanted you to know that." He shrugged his shoulders while he fidgeted with his fingers. He began walking backward out of the cul-de-sac.

"Are you going to see him now?"

He nodded.

"Good," she said, eyeing him. She was actually very proud of him. "You've done well, Tommy Santalesa. If you were any closer right now I'd pat you on the head."

"And if you were any closer," he said beneath his breath as he turned to ascend the backyard wall he scaled earlier, "I'd wash your feet with my tears."

Just then the sky opened up and bled rain as if a laceration had been made into those bulbous clouds above.

CHAPTER 2

"We should probably bring an umbrella," Myers said as he poked his head out the open screen door. The blacktop and sidewalks hissed with steam from the pelting rain.

Cynthia stood outside the doorway on the stoop in the rain. She had only been outside a few seconds and was already showing the signs of looking like a wet rat. She stared blankly at the constipated look on his face. She grabbed him by the collar. "Are you out of your mind?"

The screen door snapped shut behind them.

Lucchese stood at the wrought-iron gate. The rain no longer pelted but had begun to pummel.

He raised his palm to Myers's chest. "I know what you're trying to do, Doc, and I can't let you."

"Get out the way, Lucchese," Cynthia hissed and stepped to him.

Without looking at her, Lucchese smiled. "She's got moxie, Doc. I'll give her that, but it's not enough."

"I'm right here!" Cynthia's shouting struggled to rise above the hammering rain. "You can say that shit to me."

"There's not a lot you can do," Myers told him. "You can either come with us or get out of the way."

Lucchese expanded his chest, placed his hands on hips, and seemed to block the entire entrance.

Myers's hand dug into the waistband around his back. He lifted Lucchese's service revolver and aimed.

Seeing the gun, Cynthia's eyes expanded in shock.

Lucchese knew that Myers had learned something about using a gun during his two tours in Vietnam. After a moment's pause he said, "Since you put it that way."

Myers nodded slowly.

Lucchese raised his hands, palms out, as a sign of good faith and stepped aside. His eyes followed the point of the gun as Myers and Cynthia moved past him onto the sidewalk. He watched them become smaller as they descended the block. When they reached the corner, they made a right turn onto Hudson Street.

"Everything's coming up roses!" The priest did his best Ethel Merman and giggled from where he hid behind a tree to Lucchese's left. *"I think you have a pretty good idea of where they're going."*

With Myers and Cynthia gone, Lucchese went inside the clinic. After walking down the hall, he stood in the entrance to the kitchen. He looked around, saw the table was cluttered with the dirty dishes and the glasses, and saw the pots on the stove. He spotted his bag on the floor.

"This couldn't be better." The priest picked at the scraps on the table. Licking his finger, he said, *"Now you don't have to bring the bodies up there. It's like the cattle's walking into the oven for you."*

Reaching for his bag, Lucchese stopped and took a seat at the table. He opened the bag and examined the contents. The bottles were all there; the mallet and stake, too. From a small pocket on the side of the bag, he pulled out a shiny metal flip-top lighter. He popped the lid to give it a test. It lit on the first spin of the flint wheel, and then he pulled the zipper of the bag shut.

The priest opened a cupboard and found a clean rock glass. He quickly went to the freezer and dropped three ice cubes in it. With a bewildered expression on his face, he asked, *"Do you have any Scotch?"*

Lucchese flung the bag's strap over his right shoulder and left the kitchen. As he passed the door to Myers's office, he caught the tiny glint of gold in the corner of his eye. He stepped inside and snatched it off the pillow, shrugged his shoulders, and said, "It can't hurt."

"I'm touched," the priest said from the doorway. *"I didn't know you even believed."*

Exiting the townhouse, Lucchese pulled the front door shut. When he reached the wrought-iron gate, he made a left turn and walked toward Varick Street.

CHAPTER 3

Cynthia and Myers jogged north along empty and vacant Hudson Street. The pounding rain shrouded the still quiet that normally seethed within that area west of Sixth Avenue. The sky flickered with a white light and then blared with a thunder that they could feel in their bones. The downpour became stronger and came from all directions.

They stopped at the corner of Spring Street, and Cynthia looked ahead at the street sign in the distance.

"Van Dam's the next block, Myers," she said with her hands on her hips. She could see the definition of his pectorals through his white wet shirt and doubted more than ever before that she would ever get the opportunity to feel them pressed against her own.

Myers could see through her wet tank top. Her dark hair seemed even darker being wet and weighed down. Her shoulders and triceps glistened and seemed more defined. He didn't know what to say, so he just nodded and stepped off the curb.

When they reached the end of the block, they paused. Cynthia and Myers stood beneath the streetlamp at the corner of Van Dam and Hudson and looked east. The block was empty, dark, and uninviting as they expected it to be. The drab and unfriendly brick buildings that lined both sides of the block reminded Myers of the Midwestern steel and factory towns he was raised near and around. It didn't feel at all like any other part of Manhattan he had ever been in. Even the less friendly areas of Manhattan that Myers had visited all seemed to pulse with a vibe and feeling that was unique to that island. But that block on Van Dam Street had none of that life, positive or negative. Instead, it felt like the absence of life.

He spotted midway up the block that dead tree Lucchese told him about. He could only make out its outline, but its malnourished, wicked, and sinister demeanor shone through. Even from a distance, that tree made Myers feel uneasy.

"Myers, look," Cynthia said in a dreadful tone.

Myers followed the path of her finger and then he saw Tommy cut across the blacktop in the middle of the block. They watched as Tommy stopped at the building's entrance.

CHAPTER 4

For the second time that night, Tommy stood before the building's gaping maw of an entrance. In a fit, he bowed his head and ran in with his eyes practically shut. He kept his head down, moving forward, and hoped that he would come out on the other side quickly.

Midway in the tunnel, he slammed hard into something, then stumbled back a step and then fell on his back.

He heard the jangle of small metal, and then something yanked his hair. He felt the surface slide beneath his back, legs, ass, and the backs of his heels. His head ached and his neck was cramped. Then he realized he was being dragged. Tommy instinctively reached behind and grabbed hold of the wrist. His fingers fought for space and grip around the bracelets.

He was dragged clear of the tunnel and into the courtyard and then bumped and bounced up a short flight of steps before stopping briefly while a door was opened. He couldn't see above or in front of him because of the position of his neck and head; only behind him. He saw the courtyard and its darkened and shadowed clumps for a brief flash before being pulled again. The door slammed shut, the courtyard was gone from his sight, and he was in total darkness. He bumped and bounced again up a longer set of stairs. Before reaching the landing, he was yanked to his feet and tossed inside the loft as if he weighed no more than a toy. He rolled and then skidded on the hardwood floor, but recovered quickly.

She walked out of the darkness and headed toward him as if on a mission. He turned, hunched, and raised his hands to protect himself. While still walking she grabbed his hair and pushed him ahead at an arm's length. His feet stuttered and stumbled, but came to a stop as she pressed his face against a pane of grimy glass.

She bit into something that looked a ball of mozzarella dipped in marinara sauce that was stuck on the tip of the nail of her index finger.

"I want you to see this," she hissed into his ear.

CHAPTER 5

At the opposite corner at the other end of the block, Lucchese pressed his shoulder against the brick wall and peered down the street. He watched Myers and Cynthia approach in crouched positions and scurrying movements toward the entrance of 50 Van Dam. They stopped and appeared to exchange words between the sickly tree and the tunnel before them.

Lucchese's eyes went to the tree. It looked like some abstract, deformed, and headless crucifix. Its stem, at its widest point, wasn't more than the diameter of a barstool. It stood, Lucchese guessed, somewhere between twenty and twenty-five feet high with two large branches that extended in opposite directions, left and right. The ends of the two separate branches spread out in all directions. The very tips of these branches reached just above the top of the two-story building.

His eyes travelled back down and stopped where the two branches forked. Something was stuffed or planted there.

He watched Myers take the first steps into the tunnel. Lucchese ground his teeth as he watched it happen. The two outstretched branches crashed down and grabbed Myers. He didn't waste any time as he flung himself off the wall and bolted down the block. He watched as the branches swayed and Myers tumbled on the sidewalk away from the entrance.

Lucchese reached Myers and grabbed him beneath the underarms as the lashing branch returned. The tips struck Lucchese's back like the ends of a whip and, in reaction, he arched, causing the black canvas bag to fall from his shoulder. With Myers out of harm's way, Lucchese spun around and caught the blunt side of a swinging branch across his face. He stumbled and swayed but kept his footing. He grabbed the two branches and grappled with all his strength, but fell to a kneeling Atlas-like position. Other branches from all directions swung and whipped at Lucchese. Like a boxer on the ropes, he rolled and jolted with each strike, but the rain had made the tree wet and he lost his grip. The tree took another swipe and delivered a blow to the side of Lucchese's head that sent him sprawled out face down on the sidewalk.

Cynthia ran forward but stopped abruptly with a sickening gasp as she noticed what stuck out of the tree. Slack-jawed with a drooping tongue and with gouged eyes, Squid's severed and bashed-in head was placed on top like a crown.

The tree twisted and lurched forward and then swiped at her with a back-handed swing. Cynthia jumped back as an arrangement of the branches rattled their tips at her presence. The tree gave off a guttural moan as the tips of the rattling branches rushed forward. She looked around herself; up above and to her sides, the tree had made a cage around her. The tips of the branches made a scraping noise as they drew closer to her.

Myers rose to his feet and rushed to the cage. He circled the constricting branches and struggled in vain to find an opening as the rain flew in all directions. He stepped off the curb in an attempt to go round the tree and free Cynthia from the other side. A deformed and crooked branch rattled and darted violently, catching Myers across the face. He stumbled, and the service revolver tucked into the back of his waistband flew into the wet street.

Cynthia was huddled on the pavement in a fetal position. The branches rose and fell around her again. Her body cringed and tightened as a thin, twig-like branch sliced into her right side just beneath her rib cage. Her tank top quickly glowed red with her spreading blood.

Chapter 6

"**Y**ou did this," Aurora chided as she tightened her grip on his hair. "This all belongs to you, Tomaso."

Tommy no longer minded the physical pain she put him in. The tears that streamed down his cheeks came from a rioting cocktail of emotions within him. Horror, fear, pain, regret, but mostly sadness swelled in him like a rising tide.

Through the dirty window, he saw Cynthia's still body on the pavement trapped within the cage of branches.

"Witness the end," she whispered mockingly into his ear.

It was then that his body began to wilt. His arms fell slack; his knees buckled and then gave out. Before passing out he had the sensation of being dragged again.

CHAPTER 7

Lucchese shook it off and rolled onto his back as a branch swatted at him as if he were a bug it wanted to squash. He rolled to one side, got on his feet, and ran into the street. He picked up the loaded .38 and turned. His finger pulled the trigger and emptied the chamber into the tree's trunk. The tree gave out a hellish moan and slammed its branches down on the pavement in a fit, but managed to knock the gun out of Lucchese's hand. The gun slid along the blacktop and came to a sudden stop as it hit the curb. He darted off past the branch to the sidewalk and recovered his canvas bag.

He opened the bag and reached for the metal bone saw, but wished for an ax. With a sideways motion he brought the jagged edge of the blade into the tree's trunk. In a pissed-off state, the tree screamed and lifted its two deformed arms in rage from Cynthia.

Myers held the side of his face where the branch struck him and sat, stunned, on his ass on the wet blacktop. He saw his chance, shook it off, and ran to Cynthia. Ducking and shielding his face from the whipping branches, he gripped Cynthia by her shoulders and dragged her away from the tree to the sidewalk and stopped at the wall of the warehouse.

Lucchese backed away from the nasty tree. He stopped at his bag on the sidewalk and took out one of the bottles. He cupped his hand over the top of the lighter to shield it from the rain. He cursed and swore beneath his breath as the spark failed to take. Then finally the spark emerged and the flame grew. He lit the frayed end of the rag, fought against his own waning balance, lunged forward, and whipped the bottle with an overhanded throw at the tree's midsection. The tree's shriek indicated that if it could have jumped back, it would have. The bottle hit the trunk with a muffled pop and exploded in a splash of orange, red, and yellow fire that clung to and climbed the wood body. Lucchese wasted no time and hit it again with another bottle and then a third. The flames grew quickly and were soon above Squid's severed head. The tips of the branches burned as the tree swayed and shrieked.

Then, as it began to wilt, it screamed with the sound of a boiling lobster that pierced through the thunder in the sky.

Lucchese backed away in a stagger and stopped only when his back touched the warehouse's brick wall. The tree lurched to one side, snapped in half, and lay in the street as the dying flames fought a losing battle against the rain.

He looked away to see Myers pointing the .38 at him. "I can't let you go in there, Doc," Lucchese shouted above the thunder and rain.

Myers was sure Lucchese only fired off five shots. "I don't think you have much of a choice," he said.

Lucchese *knew* it was six. "I see your point." He eyed Cynthia huddled on the sidewalk. She was pressed against the wall with her arms crossed over her stomach. "How's she doing?" He gestured in her direction with a thrust of his chin.

Myers turned his head and was about to speak when Lucchese's hauling fist crashed into the side of his face. Everything went black.

A few minutes passed and Lucchese had dragged the unconscious Myers out of the pouring rain and into the tunnel.

"I have to say, Cynthia, I didn't think Myers had it in him, but he took quite a beating for you tonight." He folded up his shirt and put it against her side and placed her hand over it. "Hold this tight."

"You know that Tommy already went in there, don't you?" she asked.

He thought about it and made a face. "Then he's already dead."

"What's your plan?"

He threw the bag's strap over his shoulder. "I'll let you know when I come up with one." He looked down at her and saw she looked worried. "Don't worry. I won't be long."

"I know why you're doing this," she said flatly. "It's a family matter, isn't it? Your father didn't kill your mother. Aurora did."

Lucchese didn't say anything.

"The Spaniard was your father."

She watched as he sank into the darkness and saw his form vanish within the black.

CHAPTER 8

I t was the sound of music that woke Tommy as he hung in a state somewhere between sleeping and being awake. His conscious mind then followed the music notes that fluttered and danced through the air. It was a piano he heard. Some composition he had heard somewhere before, possibly in a movie or a music class, but he'd never bothered to learn the name of or the name of who wrote it.

His eyes fluttered open, and the foggy upside-down impression of that woman seated at a piano with her back to him became clear and crisp. The rain beat down on the skylight above him, and it flickered with blinding white light.

His wrists and ankles were bound behind his back so that he was hog-tied. He dangled from a single rope that was tied to a rafter above and that looped around his knees.

He had a perfect view of her profile as she sat on the piano bench at an angle. His eyes followed her form, from her defined biceps to the jangling of the bangles around her wrists. Then his eyes strayed to the slit in her dress that ended at her thigh and then down to the heels of her stilettos as her feet pressed the pedals beneath them. Her back was straight so that he could see her muscles in her lean form. Her head turned to face him.

"Does it sound familiar to you?" she asked. "It should. Frank composed it, however, something tells me you never really do listen. That's a shame. I listen very well."

Lightning stuttered and then flashed a blinding white for just a sliver of a second. When it stopped, she stood before him. Her arms were crossed and she drummed her fingernails on her biceps with a cold but inquisitive expression on her face.

Tommy shrieked.

"Shhh." Her index finger crossed her lips. "He's sleeping and I'd hate for him to be disturbed." She turned her back to Tommy and stepped to the bed where Frank lay and caressed his cheek with her finger while she looked adoringly at him. "He's in something of a chrysalis; a rather fragile state at the moment.

"When that disgusting priest died, so too did his spell of Catholic witchcraft that bound me to this…pit. With the spell gone, I could finally fly free…except for the music I heard. Frank's music. Every night I would hear it and when it came, it was like a message in a bottle. For the first time in so very long, I actually felt something more than hate. So at night when the music would come, I would follow it, and that's where I saw him. He was alone, just him and his guitar, on his building's rooftop. For several nights I watched him, and I learned what caused him so much pain."

A small spider, no bigger than a pea, dangled from its web before Tommy's eyes. It swayed and descended in a jerky movement and then landed on the tip of Tommy's nose. Aurora stepped to him, extended her finger, and lightly grazed his throat with its pointed tip. He squirmed as she tickled and stroked his Adam's apple. With an amused smirk, she placed the fingertip by the end of his nose for the little spider to walk on. It crawled along the back of her hand in a hurry, and then, as she turned her hand over, it settled in the center of her palm.

"Did you know that, despite the crown of eyes it has, a spider is virtually blind? Oddly enough, it has the crown of eyes to compensate for its lack of peripheral vision. At least that would be an evolutionist's theory." The spider walked from her palm to the tip of her ring finger. She turned her hand again and the spider settled on the back of her hand. "Being blind, it is forced to do everything by touch rather than by sight. You can learn quite a bit from a spider. I know I have." She waved the palm of her other hand above the spider, and when her hand passed, the spider was gone.

He swallowed hard to gather his thoughts and squash his fears. His darting eyes fixed on one of those brittle, plaster-like statues. It was sprawled and contorted and lay face down, but was headless. Chalk white like all the others he had glimpsed, but something about that bleached-out statue was familiar to him. Tommy's heart sank when he realized why the figure was familiar to him: because it was someone he knew.

It was Amy.

"Oh, so you knew her then?" She picked up on Tommy's reaction. "For what it's worth, I didn't kill her out of jealousy alone. There was a practical aspect to it as well. After all, the last thing our dear Frank needs now is the burden of fatherhood."

Tommy felt a knot twist and tighten in his stomach just then.

She tickled his throat again. "Again our paths have crossed." She stepped in front of him and crossed her lips with her index finger in thought.

Tommy's eyes scrambled up, down, left, and right then registered quick snapshots of the interior. A quick glimpse showed Frank stir in his sleep.

She caressed his cheek by running the back her hand and fingers downward. "Tell me, Tomaso, are you really a harbinger of my doom?" She went around him and ran a palm along his chest while she twirled his hair with her other hand. She let out a muffled purr of a laugh into his right ear that vibrated throughout his body. "You appear to have come in good faith," she said as her fingertips outlined the space where Tommy's crucifix once hung. "I can still pick up its vile scent. The fact that you removed it before you came here may be the only reason you are still alive. So tell me why you are here."

In a violent fit, she gripped his throat with one hand, while the other grabbed the back of his head and clenched down a wad of his hair. Her eyes narrowed, her nostrils flared, and her lips parted to show her fangs. "If not to steal him, then what?" she hissed.

Like a stuck pig, Tommy squealed, "I came here to—"

"To offer yourself in exchange." She mockingly smirked.

She released her grip and rounded him once more, then she stopped directly behind him.

Her hands touched his shoulders. She ran them down his chest. Propping her chin on his shoulder, she made a sound like that of a cat purring and ran her tongue along the tips of her exposed fangs.

"Each time you've appeared, something goes awry." She placed the tips of her fingers beneath his chin and slid them down his throat to his collarbone. "I won't deny the fact that you have a certain charm all your own, and that you are quite appealing to the eye." She stood up and faced him again. "But you're not Frank. What makes you think I want you?"

Frank stirred on the bed and let out a low moan.

Tommy became flustered, impatient, and desperate. "Just…take me…I'm the good-looking one, everyone knows that, and—"

Her two fingers crossed his lips vertically. She did it as though she were hushing a crying baby. "Perhaps I'm just fickle that way." She turned to look at Frank's sleeping form. "But why mince words? Frankly, Tomaso, what could you possibly offer me?" She looked at Tommy defiantly as she touched Frank's cheek. "Surprised? Oh, I've met your kind before, and you're all the same. A crass and base defiler is what you are. It's possible that in my younger days I may have found you charming and as I grew older you could have amused me, but now…" Her eyes became two hateful and seething slits as she shook her head. She pointed a finger at him wickedly. "You will serve a different purpose."

Chapter 9

Lucchese hadn't lied when he told Cynthia he had no plan. Just like he had done in the old days when he was a cop about to raid an apartment. For better or for worse, he went on instinct. He ascended the wrought-iron staircase to the rear of the building and paused at the top outside the shut door. He could feel those old reflexes of his again. From that height he could see, behind him and to his right, the tops of buildings on both the west and east sides of Sixth Avenue. He could just make out, in the distance and obscured by other buildings, the top of St. Anthony's Church.

Lucchese knew those steps and the landing he stood on all too well. He had led so many unsuspecting souls throughout the years with some empty promise of what was on the other side, but he had never been on the other side of the door himself. Naively his victims would step over the threshold and into the darkness, having no fear until they heard the door slam behind their backs.

He could hear their muffled screams beyond the door as he would descend the steps.

He knew the sun would be up within the hour and that his best bet was to drive the witch out of the warehouse by using the last of his Molotov cocktails. He knew she was afraid of the light and hoped that included fire, but it was a shot in the dark. His other goal was to rush the loft, find Frank, bury the stake into his chest, and get out before the smoke or flames killed him.

On a mental three count, he yanked open the door, and with an overhand swing he whipped the bottle into the darkness. He watched the yellow-and-orange flame twirl, spin, and descend into the darkness. He then saw a bright explosion of orange, yellow, and white light in tandem with a muffled thud. Immediately shrieks of pain and fear rang out from the glimpses he had of the shifting shadows that reeled back from the flames and scattered like roaches in a cellar.

Lucchese didn't hesitate. He rushed in toward the flames. The shadows hissed and cursed at him from the edges just beyond the flames. Safe within the flames' light, he reached into the bag for the last one of the bottles, lit its rag, and pitched it against the wall of books with the skill of professional baseball player. The flames splattered and clung to the bindings that lined the shelves. The heat was intense.

He spotted Frank's gaunt and sleeping form on the bed. Without hesitation, he stepped to the bed, looking side to side as he did so. His eyes tried to penetrate the deeper depths of the darkness that the flames did not reach. Seeing no hazard, he stood over the body. With a nervous hand, he removed the stake from the bag and then the mallet.

A section of shelf teetered and then fell over with a whine. Flaming books slid across the hardwood like doves with wings on fire. Despite the intense heat that grew around him, Lucchese breathed easy and relaxed as he placed the pointed tip of the stake to Frank's chest. He raised his arm and cocked the mallet back.

The heavy steel door slammed shut, and a swelling sensation expanded within him. He actually paused to quietly congratulate himself on his success and even allowed a smile to show. Then he saw it.

Behind the glass and the reflection of flames, Lucchese saw the face had not seen since he was a little boy. Without thinking, he dropped the hammer and mallet on the bed and walked to the man in the box. He read the wording above the man's head and felt sick. As the Romans had mocked the crucified Christ with an overhead banner, the witch had done the same to his father.

A rage within him came to a boil. As his anger flared, he saw a flicker of light within The Hierophant's eye that conveyed a subtle message. Lucchese followed his instinct to turn around and saw Tommy suspended upside down in the center of the loft from a thick wood beam. Lucchese turned again to the trapped man as if for validation. He stepped over, pressed a finger to Tommy's neck, and felt the pulse.

Tommy's eyes popped open at the touch. He was never so happy to see someone he didn't like in his entire life! Before he could open his mouth to speak, Lucchese pressed his palm over Tommy's mouth.

"Don't worry, Princess, the bitch is gone and I'm going to get you out of here," he whispered.

Behind him, the last remaining section of shelving gave and collapsed. Its books spilled out onto the floor while the fire tickled and teased the foot of the drapes.

"You fool!" Her voice rang out and was followed by a maniacal and mocking laugh that stabbed at his heart.

He turned and saw through the fiery haze her laughing silhouette against the closed door. She laughed even louder. "The prodigal son has returned!"

Black patches ascended the walls, crawled on the floor, and dripped from the ceiling. They throbbed, pulsated, and hissed as they showed him glimpses of tangible shapes and outlines of hideous things that made Lucchese look away. He gasped and shut his eyes, but was haunted and could still make out the shadowed images of hairy pincers that slowly opened and closed. Mutations of limbs dotted with tentacles and shards of exposed white bone fused from a tarantula's bubble back. It was the eyes, those countless hidden eyes that penetrated him with their hateful stares, that made him stumble and cower.

"Is this some kind of stab at redemption, Alberto?"

Lucchese felt the fingernail, cold as a blade in a winter's night, slice into his forehead. The warm blood and his hot sweat poured into his eyes.

She popped up behind his right ear and whispered, "You were so close, Alberto, so very close, but like everything else in your pathetic life, you came up short. That bastard Spaniard's been controlling you all along. Prodded, cajoled, and now he's finally got you to do his work."

Like a tired boxer in the ring after too many rounds, he swung wildly and blindly. Left to right, the stake swung in short, tight strokes that didn't hit a mark. With his left hand over his eyes, his right fist swung as his legs moved in short, stiff, and unsure steps.

"What did he promise you? Forgiveness, divinity…ha! Did you really expect absolution? He's a liar and you were so eager that you believed him. Your sins run too deep for that, Alberto, too deep.

"I know exactly when you lost your soul, Alberto. It was when you were scared, and rather than face me and complete the Spaniard's work, you decided to contain and appease me. You couldn't destroy me so you used me to destroy your enemies."

She took a swipe and made a diagonal laceration from his left shoulder down to his right hip. He stumbled and fell on top of the pile of chalk-white bodies that crumbled beneath his weight. He struggled and stumbled, but managed to rise to his feet.

For Tommy it was like watching a cat toy with a mouse it had wounded.

Lucchese spun and swung, but only caught stale air. She reappeared over his left shoulder and taunted, "All of them, dear. You brought them all to me. All that time you thought I was contained, but…ha! You tried to stifle me, keep me trapped like a rabid animal."

She kicked the back of his right knee so that it gave out and he fell on all fours. She grabbed a clump of his hair at the back of his head and rubbed his face in the mound of chalky white ash. "Don't they look familiar to you, Alberto? They should. They're all the people you have murdered!

She yanked him to his feet. "You need me, Alberto, you always have. I have always disposed of your trash. You need me," she hissed as she thrust her open hand into his chest. "But I don't need you."

Lucchese fell to his knees with his face in his hands.

"Do you remember how I killed your mother? I'm sure that image was branded onto your memories." She turned to face the Hierophant as she held Lucchese's head by a handful of his hair. She yanked his head back to expose his throat. "This, former lover, is the final result of your works."

From Tommy's point of view, her back was to him, and she stood like a woman with a cello. In one motion her elbow thrust out as if pulling on a bow and her other hand flew above her head.

Lucchese's head was still in it.

CHAPTER 10

Like two lost and frightened children searching for their mother, Lucchese's hands frantically reached at where his head once belonged. Now it resembled an open fire hydrant as the blood soared out like a geyser from the hole between his shoulders. As the flowing blood died in strength and became strained bursts, the hands abruptly stopped moving, and the torso fell forward. It hit the hardwood with a thump.

"As I was saying, your death will provide," she hissed, "the purpose you lacked in life." With the tip of her finger she made a tiny slice in Tommy's neck and filled the inside of her fingernail with his blood. She flicked her finger and the blood became a small dot on the floor. She refiled her nail from the slice she had made, and each time she flicked the blood to the floor. A line of small dots marked the floor from where Tommy hung to Frank's bed like a trail of bread crumbs.

Aurora stepped to the side of the bed. She raised her hands palms up. Frank's body rose. Clumsily he sat up in the bed, threw his feet over to the side, and stood up. With each movement of her conducting hands, Frank moved like an obedient puppet.

Tommy wriggled and squirmed like a rat stuck in a cage with a hungry boa constrictor. He watched in horror. Frank crept forward, dragging his left foot on the floor with a bowed head. His left hand slowly rose and his right arm was hidden behind his back. Aurora stood right of center—in Tommy's line of vision—while Frank was centered in the background but approaching.

The binds around his wrists and ankles popped off as Aurora's fingernails cut them with a flick of her finger. He fell to the floor with a painful thud. A devious smile spread across her face and her eyes ignited with a predator's passion as she loomed over Tommy and violently grabbed the back of his head by the hair. Tommy kicked, squirmed, but her strength was uncanny. Despite her slender build, she manipulated him with no trouble. Then with one effortless motion, she hoisted him to his feet. She clutched his throat and pressed him against the wall. Aurora pressed her palm beneath Tommy's chin and forced back his head so that his neck was exposed.

Tommy watched in horror the hideous thing his friend had become. A disgusting black shadow that pulsated and bubbled while it leered at him with a thousand unseen and hateful eyes. The shadow spread, grew, and throbbed like a pus-filled sack ready to burst.

"He's beautiful, isn't he?" she chided.

Tommy peered through the slits of his clenched eyes and saw Frank on the bed, still and at peace but then...

Frank's face rose with blackened eyes that were empty and cold. There was no recognition of Tommy in them. His facial features were gaunt and drawn. He moved jerkily and crept forward like a blind man with a walking stick. He kept his left hand extended and outreached as if it were a feeler to guide him. This hand found its way to Aurora's shoulder.

She acknowledged Frank's touch with a gentle caress of her own hand on his. Her wicked grin had grown now into a sinister smile.

Tommy, fearing the worst, struggled and squirmed even more.

And then, through his clenched eyes, Tommy watched Aurora's smile drop and disappear.

She never knew what hit her.

For a brief sliver of time, a look of confused shock registered in her eyes.

Frank was attached to her back, and she veered to the left and then to the right like a drunk dancer. Tommy watched her body tilt to one side and then fall over like a toppled statue. Her outstretched arm caught and snagged the candelabra. Hitting the couch, the lit candles transformed the couch into a fountain of flames.

Tommy shielded his face from the flames with his forearm, spun on a heel, and fell down.

To his side, on the floor and on her back, Aurora was sprawled. Her legs kicked and her mouth gasped as her hands reached and clutched frantically at the hole in her chest. Tommy, in a fit of fear and disgust, pushed himself away.

In a spasm, Aurora's head snapped forward and then slammed back down on the hardwood. Then with one last tense convulsion, her body curled forward and, like a deflating balloon, gently relaxed. Slowly her complexion changed, ashen and drawn, her hair yellowed with a tint of white.

She was gone.

Tommy's eyes searched and found Frank had slumped to his knees so that he was seated on his heels. No words passed between them as they watched her body age and become brittle before their eyes. Her figure became like a pastry that quickly crumbled and turned to dust.

In a space of time too short to measure, Tommy's face exploded into a blaring smile of happiness and disbelief. "Frank, you fuckin' rule!"

Chapter 11

Frank's head wobbled. He stared up at Tommy. "I did it for her." He looked at the dust on the floor.

Tommy rushed to his friend. He knelt down and scooped Frank by the underarms. Tommy muttered that everything was going to be OK once they got to Doc Myers.

"She's waiting for me." Frank winced and moaned. The stake was still firmly grasped in his hand.

"No, Frank, she's gone. See?" Tommy blew on the floor and the dust scattered.

The room was getting hotter and the flames danced to new heights. Smoke crept out from all points. A falling flame landed on the area rug, and within a few seconds it was on fire, too. The spreading flames reached the sheets on the bed.

"This is great! I'll get you over to Doc Myers," Tommy said as he moved backward, pulling Frank from the underarms. "I tried making a play for his secretary, but she wasn't having it." He took long strides. "Anyway, we'll get you OK…like, if Myers can't fix you then we'll take you to a real doctor up at St. Vincent's." Tommy felt the wall on his back. The exit was just to his left. "I've been thinking a lot, too, about being a better friend and an all-around better person. Not just to you, but to everyone…" Tommy looked behind him and placed his foot carefully on the top step. Slowly he dragged Frank down the flight of stairs.

Tommy noticed the stake in Frank's hand. "You can get rid of that now. You're not going to need it anymore."

At the bottom of the stairs, Tommy paused to catch his breath. He pushed open the back door with his foot and slid Frank out on the loading dock. "It's all gravy for you from here on out, bro. You're going to be famous, sell a million records, and someday you'll be on the cover of *Rolling Stone*. You're going to live in a mansion and have, like, a new sports car to wreck every week like Keith Moon. You'll probably marry a model or an actress on TV like Eddie Van Halen."

The rain had changed to a subtle drizzle. The air felt cooler.

Cynthia's head popped out from the tunnel. She called to him in a shrill voice and then said, "You're alright!"

They were separated by twenty-five feet of wet blacktop. Tommy could see her tank top was soaked through.

"Where's Myers? I need help."

She pointed inside the tunnel and shook her head. "He's out cold."

Tommy was confused. "You hit him again?"

Her eyes turned to slits and she sucked her teeth. He turned her attention to Frank. "How's he doing?"

"He's good...I mean, he could probably use a sandwich, but he's alive. Hey, you didn't eat all that food I made, did you?"

"No," she hissed. "Myers had some, too."

"All that matters is he's alive."

Cynthia had seen enough sick animals at the clinic to know that Frank was not OK. Even from that distance, she could see Frank was far from it.

Frank struggled to speak. All that Tommy could hear was Frank say Amy's name. Tommy leaned in closer to hear Frank's soft voice.

"You have to put me down."

Tommy nodded. "Oh, yeah, just let me find a dry spot because it's all wet."

Frank said it again. Something about the deadpan tone he took got Tommy's attention.

Tommy's eyes fell to the stake in Frank's hand. He shook his head and moaned something inaudible to Frank.

Weakly Frank said, "She's waiting for me." He tried to raise his hand to touch Tommy's cheek. He fumbled, but managed to put the stake in Tommy's hand.

Tommy's vision was blurred by the welling tears. He looked away, saw Cynthia looking at him with a hard look. He clutched Frank's hand tighter. "I can't. You're asking me to kill you."

Frank's hand grabbed at Tommy's forearm. "I'm dead already."

In a fit, Tommy moved back away from Frank. He stumbled, and fell flat on his face.

"I've seen things, Tommy…things that she showed me…" Frank said. "There's no going back now."

"So?" Tommy became defensive. "What do you want me to do about it?"

"Let me go."

Those words hit Tommy in the chest like a blow from a sledgehammer. They resonated, echoed, and repeated themselves over and over, on top of each other. He still could not believe what Frank asked him to do.

"There's something else…" Tommy said. "I'll take you to St. Vincent's, the fuckin' Vatican if I have to, I swear to God, but not this!"

A rage within Frank came to boil. His crooked finger pointed to the building. "I'll become what she was!" He shook his head in disgust, and then slumped down, defeated. "The sun will be up soon enough."

Tommy looked up and saw that the bulbous gray clouds were breaking up. Cynthia touched his shoulder. She had half a piece of a broken cobblestone in her hand. "You'll need something heavy to hit it with." She handed it to him.

He couldn't look Frank in the eye. "I don't know what to say."

The sinking and heavy feeling that Tommy was not only going to put his friend down, but also that he was never going to see Frank again hit him with a numbing force. It scared him more than anything else in his entire life. The tears streamed down his face. "You're my brother."

Frank said nothing. He relaxed, took a deep breath, and then locked his blackened eyes onto Tommy's and guided the pointed tip to his chest.

Tommy pulled back and brought the cobblestone down on the stake's blunt end, unaware of the popping sound the stake made as it punctured Frank's chest.

He wasn't conscious of the gasp that was sucked out of Frank, but he did see, through his own clenched eyes, Frank's eyes expand in pain and fear.

Frank rolled to his side and clenched Tommy's hand as he curled into a fetal position. He kicked, squirmed, and jerked in pain. As the pain increased so did his grip on Tommy's hand. At the point that Tommy's hand was almost numb, Frank's grip suddenly loosened and his entire body went limp.

For a moment, the world was quiet and then, in an instant, all that could be heard throughout the neighborhood was Tommy Santalesa's agonized wail renting the air.

Chapter 12

In the fall, Tommy cut his hair.

In the neighborhood, there was an amputated feeling. There was an empty spot in the window of Vinny's Pizzeria. The back lot of the animal clinic was quiet and still. From Houston to Canal, Sixth Avenue to West Broadway, and all the streets in between, a ghost walked at night.

On the last pleasant night of the year, when it was still warm enough for the older people of the neighborhood to sit and chat in Thompson Park, their conversation turned to the subject of Tommy. Although none of the people in the park that night had actually engaged him, there were rumors. One was that he was a broken man. Another said that every night he would cross Sixth Avenue and disappear into the darkness of the west-side streets. Had they followed him, they would have found him standing in front of the building on Van Dam Street.

Some said they heard he got a night job as a bartender and moved somewhere out of the neighborhood. As to where he went, no one knew. A few others said they heard he had been seen and that his bright searchlight smile was gone and he no longer tramped along by taking long strides. Someone else said he was seen one night standing in front of the building on Thompson Street. They said he just stood there and stared up at the window beyond the bars of the fire escape.

As for Frank, they said that they had heard he had gone off to Italy to see relatives that he had never met. No one was really sure what part of Italy exactly, but some said they thought it was a village a few hours' drive outside of Rome.

As the weather grew colder and the people stayed inside, the reports of Tommy and Frank faded. After a while, people didn't talk about it anymore.

CHAPTER 13

One night as she readied herself by her full-length mirror, Anne-Marie had the strange feeling that someone was looking up at her in the bedroom window. She pulled aside her window shade and saw the fleeting shadow of a figure move out of the cul-de-sac just as a blast of cold air sent some dry leaves spinning.

She bolted through her bedroom door and out of the apartment. She flew down the flight of stairs and out the front door. Frantically, she searched left and right on the quiet street. Her eyes scanned the windows of apartments tattooed with the blinking, colored, and pure-white Christmas lights. Just as she thought it was all in her head, her eyes looked up to the statue of St. Anthony over the church steps.

Then she spotted him, no more than a few yards from her, standing like an apparition.

They stared at each other for a full minute. She read the sorrow in his eyes.

Her heart sunk. "Why don't you just strap a wooden cross to your back already and take a dive off Niagara Falls?"

When he didn't snap back at her, she stepped to him and took his face into her hands and led him inside.

An hour or so passed. He was on his knees with his head on her lap. She was curled over him.

When he looked up his face was glazed with his tears. She held his face, wiped his tears away with her thumbs, and told him his penance was over.

CHAPTER 14

Nineteen years had passed when a man in his thirties stood before the soot-colored building on Van Dam Street. He laid a rose at the foot of the building's entrance and walked away. The following day a construction crew arrived. Months passed; the weather and seasons changed. All the while things were brought out of the building and things were brought in. On the July 31st of that year, the last of the construction crews hoisted a large burgundy awning over the entrance.

EPILOGUE

He came into the room clutching a piece of paper. He walked right past her, looked around her bed and then under it. From underneath he pulled out a little stuffed lamb.

He held it up so she could see it. "Real nice." His face became a disappointed scowl. "You want to explain this?"

The child looked away at her reflection in the mirror. "I have no idea how that got there."

"No idea, huh?" He straightened out the crinkled paper. It was a ransom note. Letters in different shapes and fonts had been cut from a newspaper and were awkwardly arranged and pasted to the paper. He read aloud, "If you ever want to see your lamby again, give your sister all your desserts after dinner for the next month, or else!"

"Must have been someone else," she said. "The cable repairman was here the other day. He looked suspicious. Perhaps you should call his supervisor."

"Your brother can't even read yet."

"I'm not surprised," she said, shaking her head as if she were heartbroken. "The poor boy is slow. Maybe you should send him far away to one of those schools where he could get special attention."

He put the stuffed animal down on the bed by her feet, checked his watch, and nearly choked. It was getting late.

He helped her to straighten her bow.

She was standing on the bench cabinet at the foot of her bed. She began to dance.

"I need you to be still," he said, trying to fix the white bow in her hair. "Stop moving."

"But, daddy, I was born to dance," she said as she shook her hips.

He placed his hands on her hips for them to stop. "Stop moving." He quipped, "You were born to annoy me."

The little girl took her father's cheek and squeezed it. "Oh, you're sooooooooo cute!" She smiled.

He rolled his eyes. What was the point in getting angry with her?

He stepped back and scrutinized her appearance. She looked perfect in a little white dress and patent-leather shoes. She was quite a pleasant sight.

There's no way this kid came from my loins, he thought.

"Father, oh, father," the little girl said in her best effort at a British accent. "Your hand, please."

She stood with her arm extended, head turned up with her nose in the air.

He shook his head as he took her hand. She stepped off the bench. The top of her head barely reached the height of his stomach. "Come along, my good man, or we may be late."

"Your birthday is in two weeks. Have you decided what you want?"

"Yes," she declared. "A baby elephant!"

A baby elephant, he thought, *why am I not surprised?* "Where would you put it? They get big."

"Exactly!" she said with a raised index finger. "Which is another reason for us to get rid of the insect. We could put it in his room."

"I've asked you before not to call your brother an insect."

"But he is an insect, daddy! He's always creeping around, he smells, and he makes too much noise."

"First of all, he's only three. Second, he doesn't smell, and lastly, you made more noise at his age." *Why am I arguing with a six-year-old*, he thought. "You're not getting a baby elephant!" he snapped in a fluster. "We're going to be late."

They were by the front door of their apartment. He gave himself a final once-over in the mirror.

"You look very distinguished," she said. "Come along. We must get going."

They waited some time for the elevator.

"You seem nervous. Is everything alright?" she asked.

"Just a touch of anxiety."

The elevator doors, in the lobby, split open. Hand in hand, the man and his daughter stepped out.

The doorman, seeing this, waved to the little girl. "Don't you look beautiful? Just like a princess!"

She pointed her nose in the air and said, "Thank you, Renaldo. Have a fine evening."

The doorman looked to the father with a half-confused, but amused expression.

The girl's father shrugged his shoulders.

She stepped out of the building into the humid August air. She inhaled deeply. "Ahh, what a splendid evening."

He took her raised hand and they walked.

They had gone a few blocks. The sidewalks were nearly empty as they walked. Even the tunnel traffic on Varick Street was light.

"And over here..." He trailed off.

The girl let go of her father's hand and sprinted ahead. She raised her arms like the wings of an airplane and began to spin. Then she filled her lungs and, in her best operatic voice, bellowed, "I was born to sing!"

Her actions interrupted the walking tour of his youth.

She turned around and looked at the spot he was staring at. She rolled her eyes. "I know, I know. This is where you and Uncle Moe and Uncle Frank used to play handball. It's also where you met Mommy."

"I've known your mother since the second grade," he said.

"Speaking of mother," she said. "She said a veterinarian and his wife will be joining us for dinner. She said their two daughters will be with them."

"They're both veterinarians, but that's right."

"Will they play with me?"

"The daughters?"

"Yes."

"I don't think so, sweetie, they're teenagers."

"Oh," she said, bothered by this. "That means I'll have to spend time with the insect...my brother, I mean."

"You'll be sitting next to him."

"Woe is me," she said, shaking her head.

"What was that?"

"Oh, nothing." She cleared her throat. "Will you open a third restaurant and then a fourth?"

"This one hasn't opened yet. One at a time."

"Are we rich?"

"We're comfortable."

"Like Uncle Moe?"

"Uncle Moe's loaded. Successful record producers usually are."

"I still don't understand the name of this new restaurant. Why not just call it Santalesa's Two or New Santalesa's or Santalesa's West or Santalesa Does-It-Again...or something."

He stopped, thought it over, and stared at her. "Because I named it after your Uncle Frank."

"He died before I was born," she said as if reciting a fact. "How did he die?"

"I've told you this before."

"Tell me again."

"He was sick, sweetheart, very sick."

She noticed her father's eyes drift and go somewhere else. "I'm sorry. I've made you sad." She touched his wrist.

He looked at her for a moment and then smiled. "No, you've made me very happy." He took her hand again. "If we're late your mother will kill me."

They took a shortcut by cutting through a parking lot to the rear entrance, and entered through the kitchen.

They were gathered in the dining hall at a large table. A dark-haired, dark-eyed Puerto Rican woman in her mid-forties sat next to her husband, an older white man with a youthful face, blue eyes, and hair that was more gray than blonde. Two teenage girls with the features of both of them sat to their sides.

There was an empty seat at the table. On the plate, where food should have been, was an unopened fifth of whiskey. At the foot of the vacant chair was a dog's dish.

Tommy, dressed in his white apron, stepped outside at the front of the restaurant on Van Dam Street. He held a glass of red wine. He stared at the restaurant's awning and the large brass number 50 over the door.

He raised his glass. "To you, Frank." A tear welled up in his eye and ran down his face.

"Hey, you're crying!"

He looked down to see his daughter looking up at him with a pointed finger.

"No I'm not."

"Are too."

"I think I've got a speck of caper or pepper in my eye and it's just tearing up is all."

She looked to the awning and shook her head. "I still don't get it."

Written in white cursive lettering on a deep burgundy awning, it read, *Balistrieri.*

"Come on, Frankie," he said, taking her hand. "Everybody's waiting for us inside."

About the Author

Andrew Hernon was born in Manhattan's now-closed St. Vincent's Hospital and raised in Queens. He later lived on Van Dam Street from 1995-2002.

He is married and has a daughter. *In the Shadow of St. Anthony* is Hernon's debut novel.

44584196R00121

Made in the USA
Middletown, DE
11 June 2017